CONCRETE DREAMS

Manic D Press Early Works

Also from Manic D Press:

Poetry Slam:
The Competitive Art of Performance Poetry

Signs of Life:
Channel-surfing through '90s Culture

Beyond Definition:
New Writing from Gay & Lesbian San Francisco

Revival:
Spoken Word from Lollapalooza

CONCRETE DREAMS

Manic D Press Early Works

Jennifer Joseph
Editor

Manic D Press
San Francisco

Thanks to all of the early Manic D authors whose talent and personal flair contributed so much to the strength of this company. And thanks to Ron Turner and Last Gasp, our first distributor.

Published with the generous assistance of the California Arts Council. Printed in the United States of America.

Production assistants: Lori Noll and Vivien Drabkin
Cover design: Scott Idleman/Blink
Interior artwork: Jon Longhi (*12 Bowls of Glass, Bums Eat Shit, Standing In Line, Drugs, Zucchini*), Jennifer Joseph (*Bodies of Work, Solitary Traveller, Into the Outer World, Night Is Colder Than Autumn*), Tamar Cohen (*Acts of Submission*), Jason Storey (*She Knew Better*), Janet Flemer (*Now Hear This*), Rene Castro/ Alberto Maxwell (*Corazón del Barrio*).

Library of Congress Cataloging-in-Publication Data

Concrete dreams : Manic D Press early works / Jennifer Joseph, editor.
    p. cm.
 ISBN 0-916397-75-0 (trade paperback original : alk. paper)
 1. Literature—Collections. I. Joseph, Jennifer.
 PN6010 .C64 2002
 810.8'006—dc21
                  2002002615

Dedicated to the memory of
Sunday nights at the Paradise Lounge
1988-2001

Contents

Preface   13

ACTS OF SUBMISSION   Joie Cook

Submission   17
Long White Halls   18
Rear View Mirror 1959   18
Mournings   19
The Dream Thief   19
The Pause   20
Anima   20
The Exchange   20
Gravity's Last Call   21
New York City   22
Baltimore Exile   22
Raleigh   22
Driving West   23
Between Sets   23
Specs 1:33 a.m.   24
Rendition on a Lost Theme   24
Insectlopedia   25
Chop Suey and Bad Fortune   25
They Want You Like That   26
Treadmills and Cliff Hangers   26
Modern Exits   27
Jessica   27
Chemistry   28
As the World Ends   28
Explanations   29

12 BOWLS OF GLASS   Bucky Sinister

12 Bowls of Glass   33
Tipper Gore, Are You Going to Ban My Kitchen?   33
Kissprints   34

Blackbirds   34

Strawberry Squirrel Brains   35

The Nature of Our Relationship   36

Breaking the Pact   36

Trying to Forget   37

Alone   38

Bleeding for the Late-Night Bus   40

A Special Bus   41

Venice Beach Strays   42

Jukebox Eyeballs   42

BODIES OF WORK   Nancy Depper

The Judas Window   47

Height   48

Eighteen Hours Without You   49

Hamlet Mouth   54

Eight Mulatto Daughters   56

Phil Vincent   57

Girl's-Eye   59

Double Dip   62

BUMS EAT SHIT   Sparrow 13

Bums Eat Shit   65

Survivor   67

Cocaine Pantoum   69

Clinical   70

I Was Lost   71

Ghost Games   72

Girls Night Out   73

Evil Queen on Monday Morning   73

Two A.M. in an Arco Station   74

Discrimination in Au Coquelet   74

SOLITARY TRAVELLER   Michele C.

Grey Drizzle   79
Pull In on the Train   79
Biking is Anarchy   81
Even Before She Arrives   83
Women Have All the Responsibility   85
Five Hours Alone   86
Recovery Program   88
The Mission   91

STANDING IN LINE   Jerry D. Miley

Dim Light   96
As We Left The Mission   96
Old Stew Tramp   96
Memories   97
Observation Twenty   98
Man Nearing Old Age   99
City's Homeless   99
Broken Men   99
Snaking Line   100
Two Mission Story Poems   100
How Poor People Meet   101
The Shirt   102
Thoughts From A Broken Man   102
While It Is Warm   103
Walked Out   104

SHE KNEW BETTER   Wendy-o Matik

For What Little It's Worth to You   107
Hiding the Passion   107
Crack-Child   108
Ever Thought About It   109
She Says   110
Satisfaction   111

He Scares Me   112
Cold Chill   114
What Little I Had Left   115
Left Inside   115
She Moves Me   116
Paradox   117
Fragmented Women   119

INTO THE OUTER WORLD   David Jewell

Into the Outer World   125
She was Gone   125
Birds Fly Free   126
Machine   126
Fist of Innocence   127
Frozen Shadow   127
The Closet   128
Too Much   128
Winter Night Oblivion   129
The Channel   129
He Wanted to Talk   130
My Love is a Python   130
Stoplight Skull Fracture   130
The Guilt Monsters   131
Sundown City   132
I've Forgotten Everything   132
Sleepy Dawn Surrender   133
Birds Outside   133

DRUGS   Jennifer Joseph

Wet Sheets   137
Federal Express   137
Lou Reed   138
Balloons   138
First Chapter   139
Luciano   140

This Is For   141
Beauty and Sadness   142
Nine Seven Six   142

NIGHT IS COLDER THAN AUTUMN   Jerry D. Miley

Disillusion   145
Picture   145
Night Is Colder Than Autumn   145
Checkered Suitcoat   146
The Irish Tenor   147
Nobody Wants to Remember the Street   147
The Child Star   148
Who Is Putting Her Up to This?   149
Crazy   150
How Often   150
Hopping A Boxcar   151
Written Prior to 8 P.M. at the Café Babar   151
His Dad's Old Car   152
Hitchhiking Through   153
Wisdom's Well   153
A Step Away   155

NOW HEAR THIS   Lisa Radon

Claustrophobe   159
The Girl With the Eight-Track Brain   161
Lost and Found   163
Reality World   165
Dear Barbie   167
Weirdos and Freaks   168
Apathy to Go   172

ZUCCHINI AND OTHER STORIES   Jon Longhi

Bigfoot   177
Pascal   177

Two-Headed Heifers   178

Hip Bones   178

Some Orgasm   179

A Current Affair   179

Fish Tale   181

You Should See How Many People Think They're Related To
    Dead Joneses   182

CORAZON DEL BARRIO   Jorge Argueta

Oda al Café La Boheme   195

Jaime   197

Miguel Perez   199

Alfonso Texidor   201

Oda a Benjamin Ferrara   203

Jorge Rivera   206

Victor Manuel   208

Don Jose   210

Ricardito   212

Amilcar Carillo   214

Robinson Tapia   216

Corazón del Barrio   218

PREFACE

Between 1989 and 1994, Manic D Press published eighteen photocopied-and-stapled books of poetry and fiction for twelve writers active in the spoken word scene. For the most part, I met these writers at the weekly readings held at the Paradise Lounge and the Cafe Babar. Listening to their work was always enjoyable.

The crowds at the readings were incredibly diverse: homeless poets, well-off writers, women, men, transgendered, straight, queer, young, old, and from every cultural background imaginable. I thought, 'Hey, wouldn't it be great to do some cheap easy chapbooks that writers could sell at the readings and make some beer money?'

Each little book was priced at a few dollars and it was swell. The readings were packed. Books were sold and traded. There was plenty of great writing and camaraderie. It was a pretty cool scene. People were self-publishing and there was a bunch of happening independent presses cranking out photocopied-and-stapled books for the local scenesters. Much fun was had.

Like any scene, there was an ebb and flow—the Babar closed and so did the Paradise eventually. People drifted off, left town, moved on. But the writing still stands as fresh and beautiful and unique as it was the day I first came across it, and now it's my pleasure to introduce most of those early little books in a single volume. Twelve voices with twelve visions... happy reading!

Jennifer Joseph
San Francisco

Acts
of
Submission.

Joie Cook

manic d press

ACTS OF SUBMISSION
Joie Cook
(1990)

dear poetry editor:

submission.
the act of.
this is the process.
examine my words.
my arrangement of words.
choose them.
deny them.
submission.

truly,

JOIE COOK

LONG WHITE HALLS

when i was small
hospital rooms were larger than fields
where sunlight touches grass;
at arms length was an opera
embedded in sterile sheets,
waiting for a conductor

implanted in my buttocks
were miracles of science,
injected by nurses
who tranquilized children

syringes filled with voices
saying she-will-be-out-soon
lined the walls of my room
as my father sat for days
with his book on modern jazz,
waiting for the opera to begin.

REAR VIEW MIRROR 1959

there used to be a line
i'd always see it on the way to church
men waiting for soup
and i think they were dressed similarly
in torn trousers
with greasy hair
with thunderbird breath
and i would peer through the back window
of a very large chrysler
and pretend not to see them
my grandmother told me the poor
have to wait in lines
have to ride buses
have to clip coupons
have to wear used clothing
have too many children and pets
i'd always pretend to be listening
even if i was thinking
about crabbing on the chesapeake
she couldn't tell the difference
she was a gladiator of pinellas county

waxing emerald autos and bracelets
making no excuse for wealth
it was hard to tell the difference then.

MOURNINGS

this is my breakfast:
methedrine and a six pack.
my head sunk back into pillows
and decided.
i have no control.
many friends have died.
apparently from self abuse.
i hear their sagas
on the radio.
living memorials. tributes.
and the crowds come out for
death!
they like it as much as i do.
never mind.
morning has begun.
the pace has hastened.
i must work now.

THE DREAM THIEF

he sermonizes through storms
armed with rife directions,
that no miniature hot heaven
will consume us;
but each grotesque sequence
of our survival
suggests decay of expectations
and smaller windows to look out of;
he says rooms are silent tombs
of restless night tribes,
that poison feeds on thoughts of gypsies,
that my love ticket has finally expired,
and will leave me blinded
at the end of damp galleries.

THE PAUSE

it could begin with an eyebrow
raising,
that initial pang of desire,
entering a room
with one hand in pocket,
lips wanting more than poetics;
it could be traced
to a gesture,
motion,
word:
precedents for two lovers
intertwined

as it continued, it waned on
there were forgotten beginnings:
which signal was green and when?

thirty years later
you stand in a subway
someone flicks a cigarette,
and there you are,
remembering

ANIMA

he is a night tattoo
  unerasable
      forever etched on my limbs
          unforgiving of biology

THE EXCHANGE

I shifted nightclub eyes
into your sandbox.

These being interior times,
you should be inside me,
I thought.

Through dilated pupils,
you sifted my words
as cautiously as stones
guard a riverbank.

Our next move was unarranged,
as if a human ocean
had swam the Red Sea.

GRAVITY'S LAST CALL

By the time we get to Paris,
I will be holding a glass figurine
Filled with an unidentifiable liquid
Homosexual pygmies will have
Colonized the moon
The transamerika pyramid
Will have lost its erection

By the time we get to Paris,
It will not be there,
Having merged with the greater continents
French will not be spoken,
Only Swahili
Goodyear blimps will carry
Cyanide balloons above
The grey horizon

By the time we get to Paris,
There will be no such thing as poetry
Literary archives will be buried
Under the stoned surface
Of the Folies Bergiere
As lovers hold each other
In oxygen tents
Sucking chablis through plastic straws,
Staring,
Constantly,
Towards Pluto.

NEW YORK CITY
AUGUST 1982

i hear police sirens
and see your crumbled love poem
in the see-thru garbage sack

a perpetual vision haunts me:
my head is being crushed by a thousand motorists
on the long island expressway
as i gasp
for one last
peep at
the world trade center

BALTIMORE EXILE

wedged between insomnia and dishrags
the call comes
always the night crew
customers with impatient glances
and taxi's outside waiting
while the kitchen
serves soup
and the tables become cause
for psychotic behavior
always ticking away
are the hours
stripped like the tablecloth
poured into your routine
as you silently ache
for hills and familiar tables
in other cafes
of the west.

RALEIGH

the south spews blood
from its drinking fountains

hands raise but tremble alone

smiles disguise rage

fast food parlors,
blatant reminders
of a no change
change

diet soda and subminimum wage,
the south sweats
like a pup in heat
as we cross the mall,

future battleground.

DRIVING WEST

my thoughts
bear no resemblance
to the sky at dusk
when new mexico and arizona
collide
to form
the most erotic cactus

BETWEEN SETS
(for Frank Morgan)

Opening notes
Hardcore as Bird playin joints
In coast to coast meter
    Dressed down notes
Pleasin sweet smooth skin poppin blues
Alto sax payin dues
For old blood
  New shoes
    High hats
      Front row seats
Battin ten thousand orgassed

Hyperemoted sounds
Struck at home base
Stretched out mainline
Down to a steel blue spotlight
Lifetime vision: JAZZ

SPECS 1:33 a.m.

these walls
exposed to human sorrow
have seen collapsed veins
of icons playing
win or die with confucius
at the bar:
have known legends
and dopers
and mythical healers
with plans to escape
their sentiments;
these walls
hunger
for
us
all

RENDITION ON A LOST THEME

the absence of it
brings humorless dawns,
television reality
bought and sold into black and white
standard
the absence of it
leaves life unbalanced as a catwalk,
tipping on both edges,
afraid of the orchestration
at the bottom
the absence of it
tells of the dangerous walls
four of them

moving slowly toward a skeleton's form
like the visitors at the smithsonian
approach the stegosaurus remains.

INSECTLOPEDIA

she's a chameleon,
that girl:
slithering into
new data
with style,
fashionably becoming
the charming aphid of the evening

like a lizard,
she glides through conjecture
to debris
with aspiring silverfish
climbing kitchen walls

her friends, the mantis twins,
know she is just pretending
to be vermin
because it is that time
of the year again
when boll weevils
are seldom seen
in the company of cockroaches.

CHOP SUEY AND BAD FORTUNE

three
there are three of us
I'm always searching he says
through trash cans
and alleys
unconscious of stares and strangers
just one small wish he tells me
nothing spectacular or glamorous:

to sit in the most crowded restaurant
in town
without feeling threatened
by knives,
guns
or
rumors.

THEY WANT YOU LIKE THAT

there's always a crowd to destroy
yourself in
george told me: they want you like
that: worn, drunk, depreciated,
mumbling to concrete in search
of a bottle or one last handout
they want you like that:
breathing fire into someone
else's lust but all alone;
put on remote control
by other peoples saviors
they want you like that!
hurting in napa with a tube
up your ass,
jaundiced eyes and green teeth
they want you like that!
burned out at thirty
buried at forty
crying tears that no one sees
'til the pallbearers
put the final dust
in the dampness:

cold/flesh/ZERO.

TREADMILLS AND CLIFF HANGERS

i float on the edge of an abysmal canyon
too deep yet cut like a diamond
from peasant hands

jarred into another fortune
tickets to europe are temporary answers
troubles dissipate sooner
fuck me in asphalt sheets
paris, amsterdam,
you smell different there
america is fading from your memory
slowly my eyebrow raises in smugness
you will not emerge a prince
there's an angle to this
it's a talented recollection
turned into blown out candles on halloween
where makeup drips, mascara runs
dreams end and die
fortune, never
the motel was the answer, temporarily
i have no clue
as to where
the rest
of history
lies.

MODERN EXITS

he loves in darkness,
mysteriously,
where sheets are damp
from spilled drinks
and false moves;
where women
are like windows:
translucent
and easy
to escape from

JESSICA

the halo lifted
from my daughter's brow
turns dust to gold

in her sleep
the magi wins smiles
from a flagrant princess
swept away from the funny sadness
of the larger crowd

could daydreams be captured
so perfectly
in this light?
at this distance?

and how many hours must pass
before the halo is tarnished?
the magi disappears?
the princess emerges a jackal?

CHEMISTRY

this carnival of doubt
leaves scars too deep
for sutures to reach
left open they bleed
turning glassy carpets
to scarlet need
i am lacking the essential things;
only my tears have substance.

AS THE WORLD ENDS

when quicksand envelops the earth,
sucking the ocean
into the desert,
my ticket out
will be a well-stocked schooner,
filled with every pharmaceutical
known to science

EXPLANATIONS

every poem
is
a
bank account
accumulating
interest
in
an existential
mutual
fund

every poet
is
a
meter maid
ticketing
the drivers
of mainstream

every reading
is
a
virgin
popping
its cherry
on
center
stage

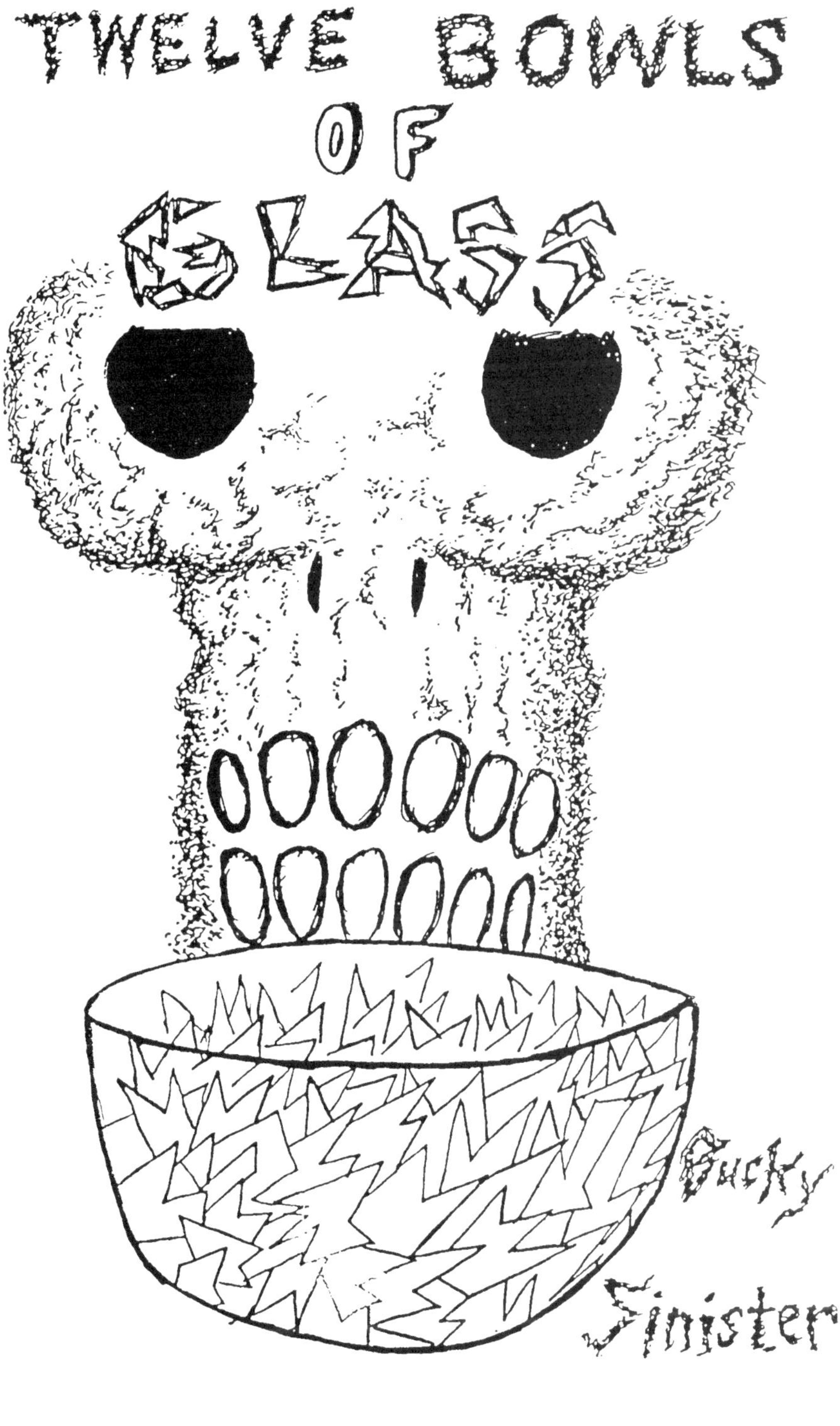
TWELVE BOWLS
OF
GLASS
Bucky
Sinister

12 BOWLS OF GLASS
Bucky Sinister
(1990)

12 BOWLS OF GLASS

When the light bulb I am changing
slips through my fingers
and explodes in the sink

like a dream I once had for myself
that was shattered the same way by reality

I turn the faucet
and watch the water take the tiny frozen spasms of glass
down the steel throat of the sink
because I want the sink to feel like I do.

They say you have to eat twelve bowls
of the leading brand cereal
to get the nutrition you get from one bowl of Total.
Maybe you have to eat twelve bowls of glass
to feel what you get from one bowl of life.

It's a wonder we all aren't screaming
like madmen in our sleep.

TIPPER GORE,
ARE YOU GOING TO BAN MY KITCHEN?

if my faucet dripped backwards
i wonder if i could hear
satanic messages

and since i am used to sleeping
with hair in my face
when cockroaches crawl across my face
in the night
i do not feel it
or wake up

and i fear one night
they will form a pentagram
and dance around my bed
to the gehenna-drumbeats
of water droplets.

KISSPRINTS

I was in a restaurant with a mirror for one wall
and this lady kisses the mirror.

I had never seen anyone do this in public
and when she did it again I started to laugh.

She turned around and said "What?"
and I said
"Do you kiss the mirror when you're alone too,
or just when you're in public?"
She said when she was alone too,
and not only that she had kissed a mirror,
but her toaster, also,
which burned her lips.

People talk about how homeless people
and others
that talk to themselves are crazy
but the real lunatics are the ones with
mirrors and toasters
and bread to put in their toasters
and walls to hang their mirrors on
and lipstick with which to leave prints
on reflective surfaces.

If you crazies have to kiss something, kiss one of us:
we will feel it
it will make a difference
some of the clouds will go away
and maybe a few of us
will even quit talking to ourselves.

BLACKBIRDS

Two blackbirds
    sitting on a power line,
    smoking a cigarette,
    and one says to the other
        "Hey, man, let's make like the humans:
        let's fly so low to the ground,
        let's live in their houses

and eat from their tables."

And with that,
    he flicked the cigarette butt
    into the rear seat
    of a convertible parked below
    and they watched as the upholstery
        caught on fire.

And the other says back to the one,
    "No, man, you got it all wrong:
    we should see how high we can fly,
    what altitudes we could reach,
    we should try to fly through
        the hole in the ozone layer."

And with that,
    they started to argue.
    They fought and fought
    and filled themselves with hate
    until they became so human
        they electrocuted themselves.

STRAWBERRY SQUIRREL BRAINS

Sitting in my apartment
listening to my hair dry
on a Saturday
and the only other sound
to distract me
from thinking about you
is the incense
burning a high-decibel strawberry.
I want to be with you now
I want life to be like it was
when we ate Concord grapes
and pretended they were
squirrel brains
but you are in L.A.
and I am in San Francisco
and until one of us changes
I will be waiting for you
with a leaky faucet

and unpacked boxes
to keep me company.

THE NATURE OF OUR RELATIONSHIP
(for Alexis)

The reason we never worked out
was due to the nature of our relationship.

I could equate it to a deer
looking into the headlights
of an oncoming Buick.

We gazed at one another in fascination,
blind to impending disaster;
if we had stayed together,
we would have been another roadkill.

But what I never have decided is
who was the deer and
who was the Buick.

BREAKING THE PACT

As two rats struggled to eat one another
in the coldwater dripping darkness of the kitchen

Two electric-eyed pactmakers sat in the living room,
quiet as a burnt-out light bulb,
chain-smoking cigarettes from the same pack,
lighting them with the candle that sat
between them on the floor
and screamed out the only light in the apartment.

As butts were extinguished in the carpet,
each one stared at the other
with more and more ferocity and enthusiastic disgust.

And when the last cigarette joined the others
on the floor

She picked up the pistol
with a look of
"you could never do anything by yourself"
on her face,
lustfully wrapped her lips around the barrel,
and squeezed the trigger.

She fell backwards
but the gun fell forward
and in the light of the flame he could see
the lipstick on the nickel-plated barrel
which was not quite as red as the wall he faced.

Long unconcerned about the security deposit,
he relit one of the cigarette butts without lipstick
and listened to the sirens get louder
as somewhere in the darkness
two rats died of gluttony.

TRYING TO FORGET

There are things I try so hard to forget
but forgetting them
would be like forgetting
that I have arms and legs

and when it all gets to be too much,
my body is tired
(even though I never want to sleep again)
and my eyeballs feel as if they have gone stale
and I think to myself,
"God, help me
I'm dying in here
I'm dying in my own mind."

I look around at all the young professionals
waiting to go home
crowding the subways
and I think,
"Don't they know?
Can't they smell me dying in here?"

Maybe they do not recognize the smell of death
or maybe they cannot smell me over their own smell
of sweat and fax machines;

But I am not familiar with the smell of death either
I assume it smells something like maggots
but maybe it smells like fax machines.

I saw a girl get into a car on Geary and Leavenworth
and unlike the other girls on the street
she looked nervous
as if it were her first time to turn a trick
and I feel as nervous as she.

When I was a child, I believed in magic,
and I thought everything was magic, like
a litter of puppies,
or a plate of warm cookies,
but the first time I saw a magician
my parents told me there was no such thing as magic
and that it was all a trick

and now I know everything is a trick
but I do not know how to turn any of them.

"A good magician never reveals his secrets,"
or so people tell me,
and so far they are right.
No one has told me anything
but I have not figured anything out for myself.

If anyone knows the tricks of forgetting,
whether you be a magician or prostitute,
send me the secrets of how to turn them,
even if you have to fax them to me.

ALONE

You get so alone sometimes
you would catch a cockroach,
Put it in a bottle that you emptied by yourself,
Name it Mickey,
And talk to it for a few days until it dies.

You get so alone sometimes
You would call someone if you knew anyone
But you don't
So you change the message on your virgin answering machine
That you have only to make you feel like you need one.

You get so alone sometimes
That the sounds of traffic from the window,
The faucet dripping,
The guy upstairs moving his furniture again,
And the light dribbling of your head
   bumping the wall behind you as you sit on the floor
All turns into words
And you feel like the crack in the window and the
   snags in the carpet
Are talking to you
And you open the refrigerator just to see the light
   turn on
And all the food is quiet like they quit talking
   when you opened the door
And wait until you shut it to start talking again.

You get so alone sometimes
You feel like throwing all the mirrors out
   your four-story window,
But it's the only person who ever seems to visit.

You get so alone sometimes
You sit in the corner in the same clothes
   you've been wearing for three days straight
Making shadow pictures on the wall,
   singing songs you barely know, off-key,
Making up most of the words.

You get so alone sometimes
You don't mind the way you smell,
Which isn't bad
   compared to the rest of the apartment.

You get so alone sometimes
When you see two people talking together
You wonder what it feels like
And you want to stop thinking the same thoughts
   over and over
And you start to have conversations that happened
   years ago

Again in your head-
But this time you say the right thing.

You get so alone sometimes
That when you come into this coffeehouse
You are by yourself and I am by myself
And you want to sit with me
    and I want you to sit with me
But we sit apart and keep our mouths shut
And pretend that we want this time to ourselves
As we read a book or a paper or write in our journals
Because you get so alone sometimes
You don't think of things being
Any other way.

BLEEDING FOR THE LATE-NIGHT BUS

Sometime after one a.m.
while waiting for the Fillmore bus
the only other person around
was a girl in her late twenties
who asked me for a quarter.

She looked like she needed it but all the change I had
was twenty-one cents
so I offered that to her
which she gratefully accepted and said,
"I sure wish you could come over to my place.
It's only a five-dollar thang.
What you say?"

And even though I had five dollars,
I told her I couldn't do that tonight
and she walked off
down the unburdened sidewalk
as I sat on the curb.

The concrete only got louder
with emptiness
and I watched time crawl down the street
like a Salvador Dali clock
painted with snails

and I could've been bleeding to death
and I wouldn't have known the difference.

The bus finally came
but in some ways I feel that it never has
and I feel like a bloodless zombie with five dollars
guarding the empty spots of the world
making sure
someone is around to hear it exist
although there are no trees where I live
anyway.

A SPECIAL BUS

A Culver City bus
Filled with people
Wearing glasses
Thick as hotel ashtrays.
They are from a special education school
And they are on a field trip
To the Santa Monica Pier.
I sit among them
And hear them talk about me
Like other people do
But they do not know
To whisper.
They yell.
They are excited.
A boy named Ray
Gets off at the wrong stop.
Ray, Ray, wrong stop, Ray
They scream
And Ray orients himself in time
To get back on.
At the next stop
We all transfer to the same bus.
Ray is still with us
As much as he ever is.
My stop,
Pico and 20th,
Comes up before theirs.
I have school today.
I get off the bus,

A bit
Jealous.

VENICE BEACH STRAYS

Eleven-thirty at night
At a pay phone on the beach
I watched several stray dogs fight over something
   only dogs would understand
And only twenty feet away
   a stray human slept underneath a palm tree.
A police patrol car came by
   and the police said,
    "The beach is closed.
     No sleeping on the beach."
The beach did not look closed to me;
     no one had even turned off the waves.
An unmarked
   but obvious
   police car
    with a "Dare to Keep Kids Off Drugs" bumper sticker
   pulled up for assistance,
As a cop got out of the first car,
   woke up the stray human,
   and made him leave;
But the dogs,
   who were watching from a cautious distance,
   got to stay,
   and they figured it was something
    only humans
    would understand.

JUKEBOX EYEBALLS

Jukeboxes play their songs
Long after
The people who picked them
Have left

And many times

They are unplugged
Before they play all the selections

And the only song you like
Is always ending
Right as you come out of the john

And no matter how long
You listen
You will never hear
All the b-sides
Even if the fool
Who punches numbers at random
Stays as long as you

And long after
The most popular song is as worn out
As my eyes are bloodshot
I will still be sitting here
Grinning like a broken 45
And you'll never
Know why.

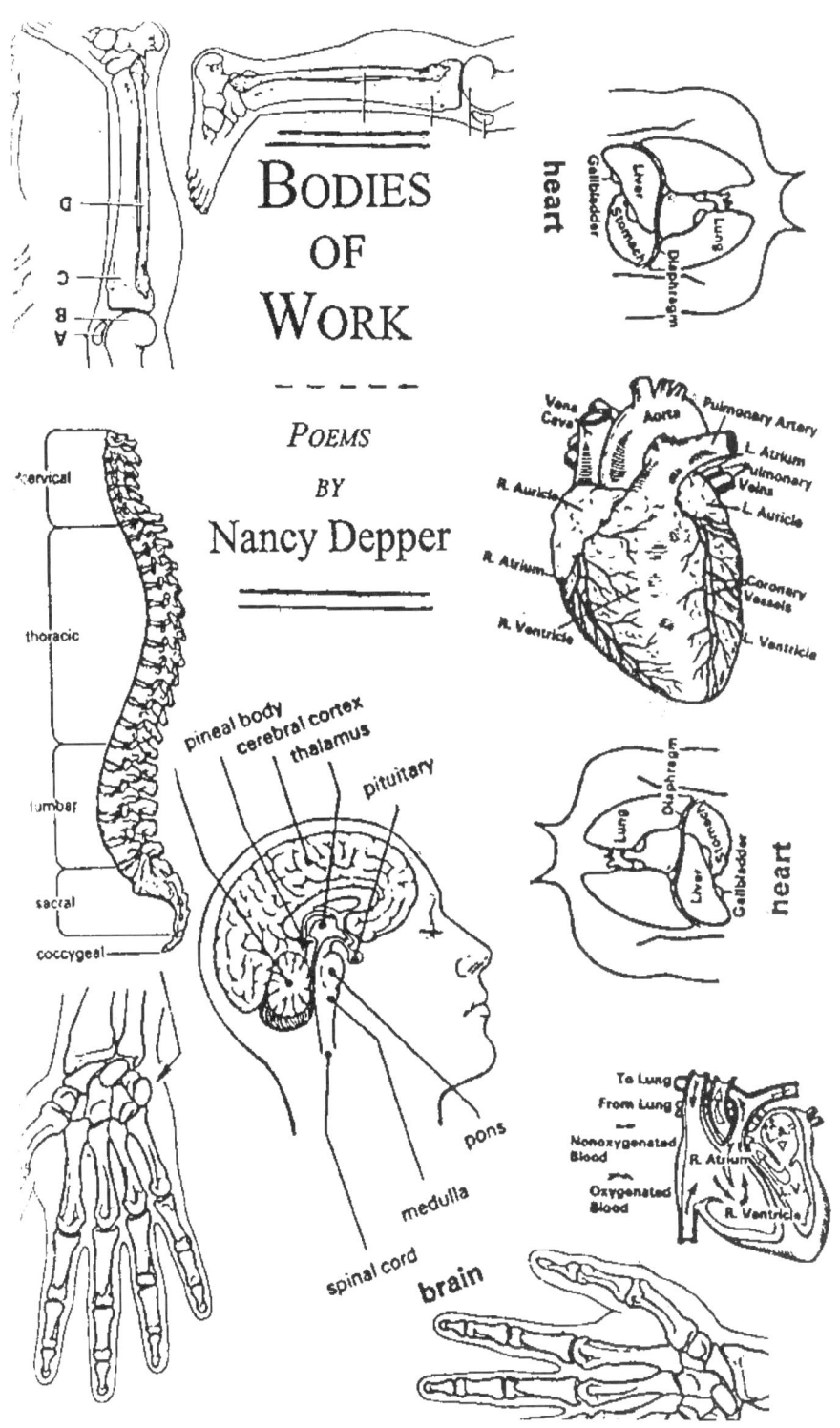

BODIES
OF
WORK

POEMS
BY
Nancy Depper

BODIES OF WORK
Nancy Depper
(1992)

THE JUDAS WINDOW

When I was 12
there was a mirror
at the foot of my bed;
I was terrified to sit up
I was curling with visions
of my face
covered with hair
and my lips rusted shut
and black.

I have always been afraid of mirrors.
They have always
betrayed me,
never accepting my own image
never reflecting me.
Instead, some woman looks out
and says:
"You missed a spot."

I have one mirror in my room,
full-length, shattered,
a wound the wall assumes for me.
My mind is dying and
the killing word sticks in my head
like a spoon,
it is not reflected,
it is stirring into me
the brains of a dog
who nipped at the death-bone
but the bone bit back.
My mind is dying
and I am straightening my skirt
in the mirror.

The Killing Word.
The name of god.
Fixed on each raw nerve
and cooked it
and I saw the skin turn red
on a hundred faces
all of them silver and jagged, and
all of them mine;
the killing word
is my name.

Formed in the throat,
I swallow the only identity
I can find in that spitball.
And I am choking on glass.

HEIGHT

My spine grew
into a knot.
I outgrew my mother
and my sisters in turn,
I smiled down
to their blonde foreheads
but my back was as
round as an egg
as hunched as a capsule
and yet that soft bone
would not break.
It turned like a useful doorknob.

They put me in a brace
a surrounding metal ribcage and
my spine twisted around it
like a vine.
I was expecting flowers
to rise.

All I ever wanted was height.
To have someone say
"She is a tall girl,"
and
"Have you seen her duck under
branches?"
But my inches were stolen,
held out on a plate
but snatched away
as if to say,
"These are not for you."

Had I been born tall
and straight-haired,
I would complain happily
about the crotch of my panty hose

at my knees, I
would not feel this
need to grow like a grind, a grip
of fingers that bend like elbows
with that length
that span that reaches
the high shelf
where the good jars are.

But not for me.
My shoulders
two of the
soft dead spotted kind
slump, like formaldehyde frogs
laying very low and
ignoring the slime
that denotes their own
lack of stature
as I do the fabled and
useless stretch:
Oh, my bones, my bones
Strong!
I'm tired of looking up!

EIGHTEEN HOURS WITHOUT YOU

I.
I don't miss you.
My walls stayed white.
My eyes stayed green.
That disordering of the senses
promised for so long
is undelivered.
Nothing is breathing
except a taut beauty
where the sheets are drying.

II.
There is no heart.
Lifted like swimming
I am more weightless
than a hundred small fish.
But I am out of water

and I am going bad.
There is no heart
in an ocean.
But my sailor is a clever shepherd,
he tends his flock of sea
and waves to me
Good-bye.

III.
My eyes are open, naturally.
If I could sleep
I would dream of blond crows
pecking my stomach down to size.
Instead, my eyes
cannot even think to blink.
I thought I saw you
looking in the freezer for vodka.

IV.
And where did we meet?
The night you lied
and said it was my poetry,
and not the way
my lips moved when I read it,
that you liked.
But you admitted it later.
It was my lips all the time.

V.
That was a cold September,
and you without running water
traded secrets for a shower.
I was the wordsmith and you did all the talking.
My mother asked if one of the languages
he spoke was "Nancy".

VI.
With an arm span that almost doubles mine
he speaks of my friendly crucifixion.
But a man who holds back,
who denied me my piercing
when it is precisely that
that I require,
that man makes me strong
when the blood in my hands is weak.

VII.
I mark the hours like some
mark days.
3 a.m. is a holiday.
It is a solstice.
The longest hour of the night.

VIII.
I am uncomfortable in my own bed.
I am remembering a breakfast,
our first,
when I was embarrassed
to swallow. Funny how
that morning's coffee
still keeps me awake.

IX.
You are not a soldier.
You are duty-free.
I read your poetry and
you read mine
and I wondered if we were
fighting the same war.
Even when you loan me a book,
I study the bookmark
as a map to your territory.
Those scraps are the details
you've forgotten,
and the cities you've
seized.

X.
I see it coming.
Dawn is the most silent
catastrophe around.
But I cannot afford sunlight.
Literally. Cheap apartments
are surrounded and mine
is always dark.
My ears slide on sheets
that held our conversation
about how you are not my boyfriend,
and you said "yet"
not me.

XI.
And I think of your mouth,
the funny way it twists
around French phrases and
how you suck my tongue
like a suicide
in a locked garage
with the engine on.
But my need to breathe
is as eloquent
as any Frenchman's kiss.

XII.
My motions have become invisible.
I am falling in love
so slowly —
I promise it will never be seen.
Because I know this act.
I was a dull 4th-grader,
I was almost held back.
And I can move like that again,
I can hold myself back.
And I'll vanish like steam
that does not really vanish
but becomes something else.

XIII.
Such a good lie
to say
"I have no memories"
no still-life snapshots
of a tall dog
with huge paws and
a twisted, drippy tongue;
no motion pictures
of little bites above my knees
and little bruises rising.
I could see them
if I crossed my eyes.
But to remember is to lie
and no perfect memory
can touch me, can leave those marks
with such gorgeous imperfection.

XIV.
You, Mister Draft-dodger,
Mister Poodle, Mister Tongue
Dance rings in a sawdust Big Top!
Pull flowers from your sleeve!
Mister Long-leg,
make squares of all my circles,
make parades of all my rain!
Grease me on the wire
I will slip through your hair
and slide you home.

XV.
I sing a song
of teatotalers.
Drunk only with sleep,
that stranger, that tease,
I tell the joke
that is Decaf.
Bitter and useless
as old age.

XVI.
"A couple of kids"
you called us, as if
we meet each day to skip rope.
As if tetherball was foreplay
and I was your hopscotch virgin.
Do you remember growing up?
I remember pretending to;
and we come together
with a clap,
we put tidal waves to shame.
I am the fountain and
you are the bounce
together, we are drooling like newborns
and coming
as surely as death.

XVII.
1 p.m. is almost Christmas.
I will freeze your vodka
and hang parsley over my door and
we will pretend.
You will come with your full sack
and stir me like pudding.

I have counted the hours
between the birds and the bees
and it is now.

XVIII.
Find me in the doorway, ring my bell!
Come, time your breaths
in sync with the spaces
between my ribs.
Homing pigeon,
come squeeze your notes
into me.
We can ignore the stroke of 2 p.m.
in favor of our own.
You can pretend to forget
how ticklish I am and
make me squeal.
I will loan you a pillow
and later we will sleep
in two small bundles,
 two bulbs that
  must be switched off occasionally.

HAMLET MOUTH

The web he spins
as white as aspirin
halfway down a throat that cannot decide
a strand of a skinny Hamlet mouth
spinning, teasing me,
he says:
Step into my pallor,
said the spider to the flighty one,
Step into the pale.

The A-B-C of him,
that language,
that fiery dictionary,
he is 21/25ths of me
and growing
now he is with me and silent
now he is gone.
He is still silent.

But he hums my torch song
When I am the siren singing
But he hums
his lips like the red menace
without one single secret,
to hide a boyish grin that
could not have seen more violence
if each tooth was a fist.
He was born at the end of a rope
and he is still clinging
to that history of suicides;
The deaths he swallowed
and never spit out
no nothing escapes his mouth
myself included
he holds his breath, smirks,
says nothing.

I would not stand for it
if I could stand at all,
But I am falling
asleep with my hand over his heart
so any blade that finds him
will crucify me
to his rib.

And like his rib, he
stretches long and clean,
without one single secret,
all bones and no skeleton;
he was never aware
of how time passes for me
how I needed my legs held
like knitting needles,
stretching leggy yarn.
Now I am a sweater
around his neck,
And when I wake up,
6 o'clock smells like fire,
a brilliant grey morning
slow-cooked by summer
and him,
with his throatfull of burden,
his swollen teeth, resting
his head on my lap,
my forgiving thighs,

his mouth in that "O";
and I looked inside for
his hiding places
I found only a miniature cocoon
and a caterpillar that was not sleepy yet.

EIGHT MULATTO DAUGHTERS

I.
I held him
like the crystal I purified
at my ear
yes and I swallowed his shadow
I wanted to find the source
his voice with my tongue
I swallowed all the darkest parts
they began to live in my belly -
I felt them like souvenir babies.

I taught my thighs
to forgive the weight
so urgently hoisted upon them
but my skin rippled at his touch
like a pond
and his fingers skipped
little calcium pebbles
across me
pebbles that slipped into my
pocket like a bullet
(but we will not discuss the gun)
pebbles that grew dark
and swollen
and rolled like blood marbles
until they settled
and fastened in for the ride.

II.
Those little brown ones
knew how to hammer
their way out
and I held them to my soft jaw
and shoulder, as many
girls as fingers, nearly,

and when I hold them
I hold the sixteen hands
that grew out of eight boulders
in my belly.
I hatched eight eggs full of bracelets
to slip over those hands
and those hands will
clap over my mouth
when it is their turn to sing.
And they will remember
inside mama
when their heads pressed
against my sunny rib
and the rays translated
into a mess of
halo spirals
that I will spit shine
as they suck dinner out of me
because
I am good food
and because they own me
like mommy owned daddy -
for a while,
the way a cancer patient owns her remission,
the way anybody owns anything:
for a while.

PHIL VINCENT

My son,
I enlarged you
until you could be seen under x-ray
bright and shiny
as a first tooth
white and jagged
you would not be softened
by my teething lullabies.

You are my test
my trial by sores
you pound my head and say:
"Look what you have grown!"
This little bead

my quiet clot,
I could roll you between my thumb
and finger, shoot you
like a pee-wee
the baby marbles I was always
in such danger of choking on;
now I am the human bomb and
this little ticker gives kisses.

But if I have rewritten
my body with language
Then I am guilty of you
You are disease
and I am a disjointed poetry;
I am the parasite
I formed around you
I live so that you might have
my life
to give for one of your own.

And I loathe this creation of mine
even as I take the credit
I am proud as any mother
who sculpts a fine bullet
nourishes it, and finally
marvels at its perfection
as it enters her eye
Yes, and you are blooming
in my brain even now
as I sip the sick stalk
and picture you tasting my death
one finger at a time
But to die at 25
is a life in exile from
a place that does not exist
And if my body is a string of words
I make up as I go,
then let my life sentence sing
sometimes in sign language
a snapping ballet
for two strong hands,
and sometimes in tears,
that plague of drowning in the
tiny bedroom that now
is mother's den,
I cry at dinner to bleed out

Phil Vincent
my homemade affliction
my family member
and I write to ink you
out, damn spot
when you scream for nursery rhymes
that I must write
because there is no better metaphor
for a head full of poetry
than a tumor
in the brain.

GIRL'S-EYE

I began as a salesman's daughter, reckless
and stuttering with mysteries
and accidental rhyme
now I am she she she, spit out
in a lovers spat
I crouch to lay that confession,
a yolk at my own heels
a yellow mouth of a baby
unmade like
my own bed in shambles,
in brutal parody of housekeeping;
Staring up at the ceiling
that girl's-eye view,
the glow-in-the-dark stars
I stuck there
remind me that night has
its sharp edges even
if all of mine are blunt
Hell, I burnt candles
and stared until even the hiss
of that light was doubled
I peeled away the skin of each day
but my naked hours are so
ugly and I am only modest
when alone
My wits have gone begging
and everyone is straining to see
eyes wide like the horribly curious
at Nana's funeral who

finally got to see
got to confirm it
and murmured
"she passed, she passed"
as if death was a test
But I was born wanting
like a short-sheeted bed, and
with that same posture, flat
and all wedges and spheres that
I was never happy with but
made do, even undressed

I wouldn't make the first move
and I hoped I looked frail
when sleeping,
I was more puppy than girl
5th grade, 4th string
reckless daughter with the
wind knocked out from a football
thrown straight to the gut;
Tonight I am still breathless
my left hand finishing
what was left undone
my left hand moving in the same
rhythm of his soft snores
But tomorrow music will stroke
back to me, too,
and getting my head up over
your knees
will be second
to getting it up over mine
my easy fist will recline
and swing me out to
my mini-Chinatown where
snap necked ducks glisten
tangy and orange, where
old women bent to impossible positions
scoop up their cowlicked young
and lead lives I cannot imagine
and do not care where I have been all
night, or with whom or
whose, so long as I have exact
change and do not stare;
I hang my thumbs in my pockets
like skinny nickel rolls, keep
my girl's-eye trained to the sidewalk

and smelling of fish and ginger,
puffed up on all this clarity
I can hear everything
I can hear my pupils shrink
in sleepy daylight
I can hear my need for
a fistful of aspirin burn
like an Indian twist to the wrist
I can hear my sister snap her fingers
to a favorite song
while she fries an omelet
I can hear my hair knitting
itself into a sweater and my skin
crinkling like rice paper
I can hear the lovers still fighting
but kissing now, stabbing each other
with my name on their tongues
I hear my stomach rumble
30 minutes after breakfast
I hear the things I didn't learn
in college laugh at me
I hear myself laugh
at the things I did learn
And I can hear my head bubble
with fever from all this listening
I can tug on the rims of my ears
like horns but those flaps
are not nearly mute enough for
my own voice like a pizzeria soprano;
It's Saturday, I should be
having a picnic, all my pots should be boiling!
And this morning on 12th Avenue
still not a genius
still uninspired and
still reckless
I climb up the stairs and back
into bed, I stare up
at the ceiling again
minus its glitter by sunlight
I shut my eyes, not
Against the day plainness
but to harvest something from it.

DOUBLE DIP

this morning I stared
at my hand
solid as an egg, with all
the softness womanhood evokes
these fingers
lined up like kisses
in a row
pulling out the tangles
rubbing lotions, blending
powders of color for the lips
all the daily intimacies
raising my hand, bringing it
down again

I did not choose a lover
last night, nor will I
tonight, perhaps, but
the work of the body
the body of work is
no one else's chore
my task my hand
lacing boot ties, dressing
warmly, choosing the stillness
of my pocket
cold fingering of the bus pass
I am still decorated with the ring
that the vendor thought
she'd sell to a child
but it fit me, a quiet shine
of support for the first knuckle

this morning my hand
lay still as a painting
not worried
(the palm line runs
like needlepoint down a long leg)
but not moving either
I lace with my teeth
let my elbows go dry
I am still no one's chore
raising my hand, bringing it
down again

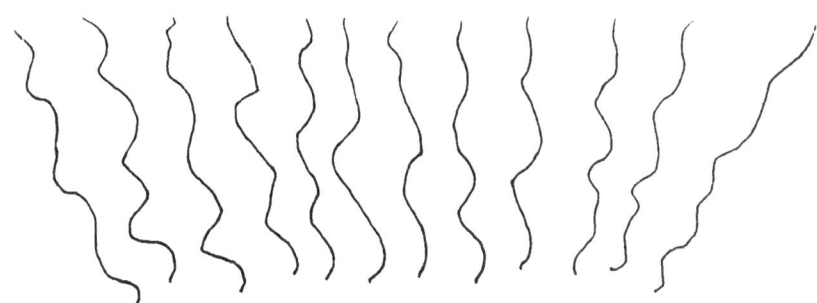

BUMS EAT SHIT

and other poems

SPARROW 13

manic d press

BUMS EAT SHIT
Sparrow 13
(1990)

BUMS EAT SHIT
(graffito on Market Street between 7th and 8th, San Francisco)

They
    sleep and stink and scream on the street
They
    expect to be fed
They
    piss in doorways and shit between parked cars
They
    curl up on sidewalks crying
They
    call you motherfucker
They
    call you sir
They
    ask you for a quarter
They
    snub Jesus at the rescue mission reeking through
    the sermon thinking only of the soup and doughnuts
They
    ask you for a quarter and call you motherfucker
They
    steal garbage from restaurants and stare in the windows
They
    lean on disgraced walls and smile mysteriously at your
shoes

and   then
They
    ask you for a quarter, like
They
    deserve to get paid for living.
They
    worship garbage gods.
They
    are scary, dirty and insane
They
    breathe rotten candy breath in the faces that
They
    ask for a quarter surely bound to wine and dope and
pornopeep
    shows, cigarettes and installments on early public graves
They
    fuck in parks like drunk alleycats just
    like the world needed more shopping cart babies

They
　　　ask you for a quarter and then call you motherfucker
　　　when you tell
Them
　　　how it is.
　　　　　　　　　　　　　　　　　　　Bums eat shit.
They
　　　ask you for a quarter and don't say please,
　　　like
They
　　　thought it came to you free, because
They
　　　get everything free, clothes and food and cigarette butts,
　　　free, and then ask you for a quarter, just like
They
　　　could sell you
Their warts
Their canes, or the needles in
Their veins, and the garbled horror movies in
Their drive-in brains
They
　　　are scary, dirty and insane
They
　　　ask you for a quarter to buy fine wines
　　　to go with the foodstamp steaks and
　　　cocaine snorted through rolled up
　　　welfare checks in the back of a
　　　Lincoln Continental with velvet seats
　　　that smell of buttermilk
They
　　　sold their souls for cigarettes because
They
　　　wouldn't work if the job was rolling joints
　　　for ten dollars an hour in an air conditioned office
　　　when it's so much easier for
Them
　　　to ask you for a quarter fifty times a day
　　　seven days a week, Sundays and holidays,
　　　at three fourteen a.m. and at the bus stop.
　　　　　　　　　　　　　　　　　　　Bums eat shit.
They
　　　are Mona whose stomach hurts all the time
　　　and Sue who writes poems on the sidewalk,
　　　RC and Pablo cast gay and teenaged from
　　　their homes, Wino Dave and Smiley,
　　　Daphne and her daughters, Otto

who got fired and Otto who quit,
lazy Mitch and crazy Swan and the other Otto,
who slid from crime to carny to the street
looking for Maisie who was saving up
to become a woman and a dancer; she
was good and you might have heard
a lot about her but the spoon found her first, and
They
are Louise whose husband would have killed
her someday, and Dallas John who rode
freight trains thirty years before
he lost a leg, and Teresa who babbles
Bible and Satanic televised syphilis,
and who got gang banged by God and her
father before she was nine, and
They
are dying a million smelly deaths
on slow dirty asphalt.
They
are fighting old wars, space wars,
cold wars and germ wars inside
Their clamorous nitflecked heads.
They
steal garbage, can you imagine stealing garbage?
They
have bruisy grabbing hands and American ancient
troubles living on
Their burlap faces.
                                        Bums eat shit. And
They
ask you for a quarter because that's all the good
You
are to
Them.

SURVIVOR

There's a white bluesman in bad odor on Market Street
Ripped off ragged ass rat jacket riffman,
Rap as long as a cigarette if you got one
Singing through brown teeth and some long gone,
Singing like the ghost of every cheap wine drunk he's ever
   been on,

Singing to drown out the footsteps of the zombie hangover
That follows him like a cop these days.
Remember when you heard him jamming
With those gospel singers afraid for their souls
Who couldn't resist the dirty kiss of his guitar strings
Like a downtown Pan with a pack of Pall Malls?
He played hard and brave as a nonstop ride
Six hundred miles on top of a Santa Fe boxcar
Now he looks like his own left shoe
And the blown out six and seven reeds
On the Hohner Special 20 in his pizza greasy pocket.
Remember when you used to hang with that man?
Panhandlers and pigeons still scratch after
The crumbs and diamond notes falling off the guitar
That's been strung with his nerves.
There's a longhair lowlife Market Street musician
Singing like Coyote for me and you
And a sandwich and a short dog later on
With every jail and onramp in California
In those crazy red white and rinse blue eyes
That watch for the cops and
gleam at the girls and
Read the dates on every speck of change in his beat up black hat
While his pale grey fingers keep singing.
There's a beat up burned out blue eyed bluesman
Creating a nuisance on Market Street
With a pot leaf tattoo on the back of his hand
Six girlfriends nine warrants and a drunk daddy, a dog who
ran away
                and a road buddy who died
Scattered out over the country (and a teenaged son living
With an uncle in New York City
Who wakes up at night from ambivalent dreams
About that red station wagon
They couldn't afford to get back when it got towed).
It's only a matter of time before they bust him again
But right now he's in tune and going good.
There's a white blues man in bad odor on Market Street
Whom nobody trusts anymore -
But when that man starts to play
You can't do anything but listen
While he jangles you like loose change
And the funky streets go cool black and silver
Till it's time to go to the doorway
Where he sleeps alone in the tattered blankets of his history.

COCAINE PANTOUM

She's praying to the Versateller machine
Eyes red as pills and psych ward bright.
God's cold copper guts pulse hot money.
Cars are staring at her. Tellers mutter.

Eyes red as pills and psych ward bright
Her religion ticks in a glass vial.
Cars are staring at her. Tellers mutter;
"Somebody had better call the cops."

Her religion ticks in a glass vial,
Her shadow chills the machinery.
Somebody had better call the cops,
She's a 51/50 for sure.

Her shadow chilled the machinery.
They had to come and get her.
She's a 51/50 for sure,
Praying for an instant miracle.

They had to come and get her
Before the manna dropped,
Praying for an instant miracle,
She got a Thorazine bed.

Before the manna dropped
(she wanted another hour of grace
But got a Thorazine bed)
She was on the hellbound bus

She wanted another hour of grace
But that's blasphemy.
She was on the hellbound bus
For asking God directly.

But that's blasphemy;
No one shall look at his face.
For asking God directly
She was bound in tight white hours.

No one shall look at his face
Cold pulse God of laws, not miracles.
She was bound in tight white hours.
She prayed to the Versateller machine.

CLINICAL

wrong place at the wrong time
denver the wrong man
didnt your mama warn you about strange men
fucked me   chokehold   half to death   backhand
i was stupid   convulsed   he came rage
only rage in him
he shot it up my ass   belly bloated terror
say you like it faggot
say you like it faggot
say you like it
blindfold   hands tied led out to the alley
theres six more niggers waitin to fuck you ass boy
shoved me down kicked my head i woke up
got loose   walked down colfax
red light stopped me   like a
cop car cop voice   ncic
youre bleeding are you ok
youre bleeding theres an ordinance
youre bleeding are you ok
theres an ordinance   the ambulance
two in the morning   are you dizzy
are you drowsy   do you want to make a statement
emergency   doctor   finger
came back bloody
stuck it in my ass
came back bloody
touched my hair
are you a homosexual
do you have insurance
do you want to make a statement to the police
insurance   the only support my parents ever
gave my travelling
twelve stitches
on the next bed
suicide attempt
drunk tank refuge
chewed through his wrists
they took away his knife
came back bloody
say you like it faggot
treated and released
you cant stay here
twelve stitches
when they got the insurance bill

i told my parents i'd gotten drunk
and fallen down a flight of stairs

I WAS LOST

Deep Creek, early April, a lovely twilight -
We lived in a shack two miles from hot springs.
I went alone and stayed too long.
Light left quick and quiet
And the trail slid off like a sidewinder.
I scrambled up a canyon wall, gibbering quietly
Because of the feud with the crystal cowboys
At the ranch a mile away.
Dark came on quick and quiet.
The creek reminded me how thirsty I could get
Out here.
That was all the sound except for the birds and bugs
Until I kicked a rock off the edge
And it landed
With the sound of me broken at the bottom and chewed by
scorpions.
I yelled then
And prayed -
We had Chick religious comics at home
And the Freak Brothers and Spiderman;
So I got saved three times,
A little louder each time,
Foaming like a Holy Roller.
But it got dark anyway
And I was still lost.
When I shut up I saw a big rock
With an overhang or undercut
Cozy to coyote - curl under
So I did.
It smelled like god's dogs
And I heard them somewhere.
Maybe Coyote sat up on that rock
While I slept the sleep of snakes in dirty denims,
Or maybe the deer bent down to kiss me or
a kitfox sang hymns backward.
It could have been stony desert fairies scuttling by
on dozens of whispery legs who stopped to mischief,
Or thirteen ghost Indians standing watch over me;

I don't know.
But I rose with the sun,
Alive, cold, dirty:
A heathen.
I made my way home
Where Mark was reading the Bible,
Larry frying eggs with Reagan cheese.
They said they'd been about to go
Over to Bowen Ranch looking for me -
No need, I said. I made coffee and rolled a cigarette.
Larry came to pick a leaf out of my hair -
It was a little red feather.

GHOST GAMES

Sometimes we'd get together when we were kids,
Cousins and neighbors with kitchen drawer candles;
Away from adults
To hold seances:
Whispering hand in hand a goosebumpy circle
Telephoning ghosts in dark rooms.
It never worked.
This was before channeling
And when a tickly cold something came down
They'd woo-ooo and giggle it away.
It made me so mad -
I wanted ghosts.

Once Sue Clark started talking in a man's voice
But everyone got scared and ran.
Aunt Shirley was drunk once and tricked us
With a flashlight outside Robin's room.
Bonnie always asked the Ouija board
Who DeeDee would marry and screamed with laughter.
It made me so mad -
She was pushing it to spell Stevie.
I took it seriously -
I was the only boy
And I wanted ghosts.

GIRLS NIGHT OUT

I dreamed I was on the same locked ward
With Norma Desmond and Baby Jane.
One night we dropped our pills
Into the guards' coffee and skipped out
To a wino hotel in Berkeley.
I went out to cash my SSI check
And get us some brandy and chocolates -
But I got into an argument with a couple
Of Jehovah's Witnesses along the way
And when I got back they were fucking Dr. Who and Sonny Barger!
I yelled Hey! but they didn't notice,
At least they hadn't forgotten condoms.
I was still a boy in the dream - I got huffy
And took my brandy over to Janis'.
She met me at the door in her tapestry muumuu
That showed Peggy Caserta and Dan Knapp being hanged -
But who's she got in her room but Junior Tracy
Trying to hide his badge under art school drag
And sketching me naked on a Kleenex!
I tried telling Janis he was a narc - she smiled
Like on the Pearl album and said, But honey
Ain't he the prettiest thing?
So I dropped a hit of acid in his drink -
Then there was nothing left to do
But hitch back to the nuthouse
Where I'm still famous enough to get laid.

EVIL QUEEN ON MONDAY MORNING

I am pissed to the tits
Stay out of my way!
I'm a fierce fussy fairy on the radical rag
And my spit can eat holes in the wood today
Go away!
Not for me the red Marie or Janis glad rags today
I am more fatal than fey.
My proper drag is Kali Hecate with a silvery knife at my thigh -
The first jerk who dares to yell Hey Faggot at me
Today is going to die.
I seethe
Perfumed with rancid jiz and bleeding magic words.

A grim alphabet of black and green jagged letters
Is boiling behind my eyes today -
What did you say?
I've got my witch tits;
A steely knife thigh
And a painted evil eye -
I feel one savage sissy today.

TWO A.M. IN AN ARCO STATION

Stan worked graveyard. He was reading LIFE
Thinking about Marilyn, when the green Rabbit stopped
At self-serve. Three men: one dark, one blonde and
one plump bearded
Climbed out together and came in the store

Moving easily and talking with each other
Across the room like it was their home.
The dark lean one wearing a golden earring
Bought eleven dollars of gas.

"What did Mike want again, Terry?" the blonde asked
when he'd gone out to pump. "Fritos and a Coke."
They bought apples too, cheese, and Salem Lights;
Stan took the money and they left, still chatting.

Terry laughed at something, put his arm
Around the blond man's shoulder. They got in
The car and drove away. He watched them go
North and checked the clock. It was 2:09 a.m.

Alone behind his clean white counter
Stan went back to his magazine
(It was a slow night).
"Queers," he said inwardly.

DISCRIMINATION IN AU COQUELET

A sexy street guy, graceful, tough as a tomcat struts in maroon
        boots and long redblonde hair that swings down over the KALX
        sticker on his blue backpack

Here come bright haired high school kids
To spend dollar bills and their lunch breaks
On pastries and colored sweet water
Outside an old woman's talking to herself, barred by the sign
That reserves the right to refuse.
Why serve me then? I'm freaky and ragged
But I'm here - with my eyes cappucino'd wide,
A dollar thirty bought the jeweled goblet
Of a medieval priest holding privilege
With the coffee in soft gold bossed hands.
I'm ashamed
So I go to the bathroom
Where three minutes into my shit there's a crass banging on the
　　　stall door and one of the immigrants who runs the place
　　　yells "Come on out of there, chief, I got customers waiting!"
Chief!
I take my time coming out - he's sitting with
A woman who says "Oh that's not him, he must have left."
She says a bum was in there ten minutes - so she
Called the manager,
Not that she'll ever see the inside of that room.
They both apologize
But when I say "Well, homeless people have to shit, too."
They look at me like I spoke Esperanto -
And I'll have my next cup elsewhere, thank you.

20 NOV 1984

1A121A121A121A121A
IMMIGRATION SINGAPORE
VISIT
Subject to
Immigration Restrictions
20 NOV 198

PERMIT
FOR A
FOR FOUR
SOCIAL VISIT ONLY F
DATE SHOWN ABOVE

A121A121A121A121A12

A442 FRANCE

CHARLES DE GA
1 0 JUIL. 1990

SOLITARY
TRAVELLER

MICHELE   C.

LEAVE TO ENTER FOR SIX MONTHS
EMPLOYMENT PROHIBITED

IMMIGRATION OFFICER
*   (2.7)   *
−8 AUG 1990

SOLITARY TRAVELLER
Michele C.
(1990)

GREY drizzle suits this village
I'd enjoy it except for my rope sole shoes
Vanja likes perfumes
tiny bottles and sample size tubes
in front of her vanity mirror
lining the shelves instead of books
her fringed lamp glows amber in the dim
of shutters and clouds, she has
her own set of scotch on the rocks glasses
in a cabinet near her bed
her father sleeps with the refrigerator
and every couch folds out
I walk through the soggy yard
to piss down the outhouse hole
my aim is improving, still,
it's tricky in these shoes
Vanja's grandfather is feeding the pigs
they squeal their frenzy as sharks are silent
cloven hooves sink into the muck
they wiggle elongated wet pink snouts,
want more food but run from my outstretched hand
Inside, Vanja wrestles boys on the floor
shrieks when they tickle, pulls their hair
I suggest she bite them
Her father reads the newspaper next door
sensibly leaves her alone
I map my progress
I change my plans
This is possible because I do not live in this village
I am a solitary traveler
the moment is mine to spur

PULL in on the train and see the ugly backside
of any town, sooty factories and houses
too close to the tracks
laundry snapping as the train rolls by
dry but never quite clean
the myth of the eastern bloc country
tells us the socialists take care of their own
but the floor of this station is a black
smudge of grime and the people sleeping here
with no choice but newspaper or cardboard
between their dirty clothes and the dirty floor

are folded along the perimeter of the rooms
one long hallway smells of feet over breath and
cigarettes, a display of mucky socks and one woman
asleep with her skirt bunched up around her waist
her tights twisted at the crotch for all to see
From my own newspaper island
I lean on my pack and write
the woman next to me gapes, dozing,
her mouth balding with lost teeth,
an enormous mole on her cheek
looking like it could crawl away on its own
some internal clock tells her it's time to go
she collects her cardboard and drooled on pillow
just before police come round the corner
I'm lucky to be awake—he tells me to get up
then I watch him roust the sleeping regulars
He squints his aim, tucks his tongue
presses his lips into a sadistic line and
He swings
the club smacking sorry tops and soles of feet
man or woman, the slower they move
the more he hits
I think it's the highlight of his job
the people shuffle away, cigarettes loose in lips,
eyes always dim and tired
one woman with a compact pats at her face
the skin is porous terra cotta to the base
of her throat where the color ends abruptly
with a harsh line - I cannot tell if she is applying this
shade or attempting to cover it
I wait with my bag at the door of the
information center
big ass women push ahead, press against my shoulder
one and a half hours before the office will open
When we are let in, there is a stampede
a crush of rushing to the next line
I am caught, Jesus Christ!
My groceries crush against the door frame
I cannot reach my backpack
a man grabs it and runs to me,
helping in this madness, I yell thanks
as he runs to his line, smiling over his shoulder,
a nice fellow
the bureau guard recognizes me
I've been waiting hours
he sends the others behind me

I am first to change dollars to forints
two more hours pass waiting in a second line
a guy attempting to insinuate himself ahead of me
I tell him, I'm next, he concedes, ok
but my waiting is fruitless
I walk away to try the phone booths
they are tombs of rank odor, piss never flushed
festering in a closed box as I uselessly dial and dial
A man whips out his dick and pisses between
my booth and the next, I give him a disgusted look
(mind flashes back to the amsterdam flasher who
ruined my whole day seven years before...)
He tucks it in and when I step out
I see him drinking at the platform bar
later, the subway system will deny the rail station
not a mark, not a scrap of litter
no crowds, no one sleeping in his own filth
timely, efficient
a proletariat ideal

BIKING is anarchy
I am not part of the reason
this earth is pierced and drained
of its fossil fuel
I am not
the demand which must be supplied
no governmentally subsidized,
environmentally treacherous
oil company makes money off my need
to go to work and return home each day
I do not
poison the air with carbon monoxide
I am beholden to no
department of vehicles for a yearly sticker
which permits my movement
likewise, I do not pay to park
great distances from the places I go
and my balls are not bound
by an insurance company's monthly bills &
yearly balloon payment
in a nation where status is measured
by the size and expense of one's car,

I have no status
in a nation of consumers where
automobile manufacturers spend billions
to convince everyone that their product
is the most reliable, beautiful,
desirable and thus, necessary car to own,
I buy none

Biking is anarchy and momentum
auto traffic is to be gauged,
drafted, cut through and avoided
traffic laws are relevant only
in the presence of traffic and the law
—that is police—otherwise
it's a matter of flow: timing it right
and stopping as little as possible

Biking is anarchy, momentum and the mind
free to wander

I imagine the earth as a great crusty husk
devoid of the oil we've killed to obtain
for the grease in this country's grating works
our following economic and industrial collapse
leaves a maze of abandoned cars,
forever parked, siphoned or left stranded
in futile lines around gas stations with nothing left
to serve or arrested in mid-right turn
as they sputtered out of fuel
multi-level parking garages transform into huge
graveyards jammed with unstartable cars &
not even tow-trucks have enough gas to move
all the junk cars away, they slowly rust,
enormous armored exoskeletons of tiny bugs
which were forced to crawl out and away
on their own two flat feet, unprotected
I imagine San Francisco as I've seen
films of China: all humanity merged alike,
pedestrians and bicyclists teeming
streets and sidewalks with choreographed
function: movement, travel, self-propulsion
but without the solemnity of uniform clothing
and the immobile ethnic mask of a single culture
San Francisco would remain varied and garish,
american and international, wild with patterns
and faces placed closer together without cars

boxed around them, we would no longer
be separated, we would be forced to see

EVEN before she arrives
and before we speak
for the first time
the similarities
are too many
I've noticed them at
third person distances
at parties and at shows
there were a lot of single
or swingin' women
boldly prowlin' the town
still are, yes
but I've never happened
across someone who presents
this somewhat distorted
picture of myself in any town
I've lived in, yet here:
was the dark brown hair
in the similar cut, green
eyes beneath wide brimmed hats
dancing, as I did at her age,
with another girl to her favorite bands
She is younger than me
and it was nowhere more apparent
than on her face when she stared
up at his antics
from a position of leg folded
adoration on the floor
and I made note:
the tattoo of the willing sucker
is the glow of her romanticism
Later I watched as she
followed him at a party
and it was obvious then
he was ignoring her
in the way he disregarded
anyone he'd been fucking
whenever they happened to be
at the same social gathering

She followed with that
carefully held expression
of bland aloofness
that signifies the hurt feelings
of a girl who fancied herself
a loner till she decided
to throw it all in for THIS one
she was Learning To Adjust to him
as everyone who fucked him did
So I watched her and felt no yearning
for her youth and even later
the clues he spoke alluded to no
intensity of connection between them
she was simply another one of his many women
He disappears, becomes a telephone voice
but the endless paths continue to cross
and meld and split in this town
and since I've seen her around
but have not witnessed any
mocking correlation between her present
and my own past, I have not pondered steadily
the coincidences of our lives
until I am reminded to do so:
she arrives on a Wednesday to
force the coincidences to multiply
She is toting her teenage poetry
of pulsing and hearts and a friend who drove her
they're in the kitchen where my co-host
pours cheap red wine into mismatched glasses
as I stand in recycled boots
center of the living room, listening
He is showing her the kid art
on the cupboards and walls and she says,
"Yes, I have a lot of this, too. I work
in a daycare center, I'm a teacher."
and I'm grinning to myself, ticking off
these amazing likenesses as they
lift and hover in the air like
word balloons over comic characters' heads
The three of them walk down the hall
and we all sit on the floor and prepare
to listen to her reading with hope for a show
She gives us little introductions
this one's about...
I wrote this one in Europe when I...
The ceiling is crowded with mental balloons

and I'm checking in my wandering mind as
she reads on, the list of parallels against the
list of his women: X number were writers, X number
were teachers, X number traveled Europe, X number
were students, X number played music, on and on...
how he could he have kept their details straight, and
did he ever really try?

WOMEN have all the responsibility
for life, he said this
on the morning of my latest
gynecological exam and stocking
of pills and it's true
although you don't even see it as
responsibility
when you are a girl
you research puberty at the library
and read novels about pre-teens
who, like you, are obsessed
with the idea of menstruation
and all its implications
you buy mini-pads at the drug store
they have no use
it's experimental like blue eye shadow
and clothes much too large for your body
you just want it to happen so badly
but you are ignorant
despite your endless reading
ignorant and surprised
at the ache of your swollen belly
a peculiar twisting gut as you
talk on the telephone to a new
friend from your new junior high school
in the bathroom your bowels
clench and spit as if all your
intestines might just land in the pot
finally it's the toilet paper
that tells you with a bright crimson smear:
you are now the woman
you want to be
women remember this clearly
forehead to knees, still on the toilet
nauseous with cramps and disappointment

shit! this will happen
twelve times a year for at least
forty years! what a dirty gyp!
take it back!
who ever still wanted this prize
after it arrived?
only babies could stop this process
of monthly filling and expulsion
this shedding of dense slippery glop and pain
and babies are no option
to a twelve year old girl
so it's one grudged week every month
dedicated to sopping the flow
with thick blue pads adhered
to cotton briefs, pads which
slide and twist sideways to chafe
as you bike to and from school

no young girl's mother tells her
of tampons at such an age
all the girls so stricken shuffle
the halls and classrooms in fear that
the nasty rag will come loose
and drop from beneath a skirt
it's a couple of years
before you buy your own box of tampons
your friends call them plugs
and they are, they do
you are free of the diapers of womanhood
and so glad, so free
you laugh at your mother's sighs
and worries about your possibly
impaired virginity

FIVE hours alone with
the neighbors' screams and
workmen's hammers else-
where clanking
electric saw shrieking its incisions
the dogs are quiet
I study latin temperament now as I once
studied the silent affliction of deserted
ghost tenements in the western addition

the noise of need is a clamorous wail
the women are cowed
the men are brutally victorious
at home and crushed by the world
the children learn by example
every one suffers
I hear the screams bouncing
from light shaft to back wall
an echo so many surfaces removed
they are sometimes too far away to help
the houses indistinguishable
along the row of insets and shadows
no one person knows
what subtle tortures lie
behind the iron gate front doors
long afternoons of beatings I have not seen
starting earlier on Saturdays
this one against that
another against the first
the hierarchy of terror shifts
as the bruised children grow older:
mother howls in the front room
voice echoes off the pavement
in wordless animal shrieks
as she shuffles back and forth
in her house dress and scuffies
it's 10 a.m.
the neighbors huddle on the front step
listening and waiting for it to be bad enough
to act upon - the woman from next door
says, I wouldn't let any son of mine
do that to me! and pinches her own
to show him who's boss -
inside the unbalanced fat boy
is screaming obscenities
fuck you asshole fuck you asshole
in cracking preadolescent hysterical rage
the children learn by example
mother howls, shuffles in scuffies
who is fat robert thinking of as he
hits his mother?
just the bulk of him puts strength
behind his blows and this is not enough
for them to act upon?
- the woman has also said, why are you hitting her?
I'm going to call the police on you again! -

but she does not do so
she waits, looking at the ground
the boy is crying and screeching
fuck you asshole fuck you asshole
his little sister looks at the ground
mother howls, shuffles in scuffies
they're all waiting
but I cannot
nearly leaving my breakfast in the driveway
I rush to phone 911, thinking
it's too much! no one should be subjected to that
and it blurs
when the children come out to play
they fall on the pavement in fights
the children learn by example
a man leaves his car at the stop sign
and breaks two boys up
they circle each other,
adjusting their sweatshirts
and walk on
the man gets back in his car
and drives away from this neighborhood
in quieter times I watch the family across
the street and their life seems too hard
how do they deserve the sociopath over-
indulged eldest son who throws awful fits
and hurts his mother? why is he so lacking
in control? why can't they control him?
does anyone need their catholic obligations?
the old man and woman made babies
to the bitter malformed end
the youngest child scoots the floor
and howls her own wordless torment
they lift her roughly by the arm
to move her out of the way
late in the evening the old man sits
rocking her as he watches tv
they are framed by the window to the street
they are back lit by novena candles
burning for the saints' merciful intervention

RECOVERY program! I've heard that story before and
I've seen it third personalized:

"She'd O.D.'d in the afternoon..."
Tubes down the throat, self-glorifying babble
she had intended the romance of desperation
but she only stuck it in cause her boyfriend did
and she thought he was cool
This was the story: rehashed and rewritten
to suit any occasion, I heard it again
from other mouths at S.F.'s liveliest reading,
later I wrote about the notebooks surrounding me
on the laps of other black clothed girls
who read "her" lurid tale over & over
"the way to heaven is dead with your boyfriend"
"speed's fun" and the living death languor of junk
redescribed was the gist of it
not poetry, but nostalgic glances over the shoulder
to the spike and spiral down of unrenown
all the half-assed detox types do it the same way
they can't let go, they're reliving glory days
or enacting the "contact high" scene in *Go Ask Alice*
she read the page I'd scribbled and had to ask
"Is this about ME?"
The personification of a cliché polling the audience
to confirm that her legend exists!
Tedious personality inventor! Psycho fiction mind!
A drama student workshop drop out
in my apartment, sifting life, creating scenes,
she unfolded like a bad joke
I found out she had fucked a long series of
Housemates in an attempt to inundate their lives and
suck them into hers
she was looking for a substitute family:
she acted out, became abusive, intrusive,
created chaos and demanded to be tolerated,
even loved, in spite of it (or perhaps, because of it)
she wrote me a victim's part, complete with tears
I'll admit I played a sucker...
She began her saturation process with telling
the O.D. Story
the ending rephrased
each time to give the most lucrative impression
if it paid to be the abused, misunderstood,
starting fresh
helplessly-obsessed-with-love-tragic-heroine,
she'd play it with those who could score
dope for her, she was ready to trade and use,
she layered her lies

The personalities she invented were a precarious
stack of cards, she was manic they shouldn't topple
but they always did
so that every former apartment was unapproachable
a new bridge was necessary
to cross the moat of ill feelings
all she'd left behind were charred skeletal stumps
she never wanted or hoped to repair
those severed relations
she proudly admitted lists of people
who no longer spoke to her, who refused to involve
themselves as far as a conversation
she bragged how she had forced her father with
hospital tantrums to place her
in some hokey schick center
for her court ordered rehabilitation
he wanted to leave her in the county facility
but she shrieked and cried and thought she'd proved
something when he gave in and shelled out
The dollars numbered in the thousands
and this was triumph enough
she didn't seem to notice she still had no insight
she made word collages of lines lifted from jokes and
songs and conversations:
she sent them off in letters home to try them out,
later she rearranged them and called it poetry
she made plagiarism and art thievery her livelihood
she cultivated short lived sympathy and crash pads
she hit and ran
When I saw one of her ego balloons
in a 12-step magazine
I had to laugh, she couldn't have done more than
found a new way to cash in, shameless
she had changed her name to protect the freak
I am unforgiving
I am her personal cynic
too hard-boiled to trust in karma to exact payment
for the crimes she's committed against me
after nearly three years I still want her to eat shit
I still want to witness the act
my grudge is sharp and metallic like a blade
my grudge is hooked like a cane
and ready to yank her ankle on the stairs;
I am always aware, peripherally scanning,
perhaps you've seen her:
she slinks, insinuating hip bones, thinks

she's being stared at, her head is aswivel
looking to see who's looking
when it's only me, she's caught,
embarrassed by my eyes... she supposes
she's always on stage
the center of some attraction
she swings her hair, squints
and jaunts away with feigned nightclub purpose
every vacant expression is hers
every shaggy betty ponytail with brown roots is hers
and the curse that she deserves
is on a short leash, cuffed to her forearm

THE mission: wait on a bus stop bench
stained rusty, old blood on the cemented pebbles
odors of puke and urine and trash
rise up from splattered sidewalks beneath
staggering drunks' flaring legs angled
like crooked capital A's
then hair faced old women fall muttering
against you on the lurching bus, clutching
with dirty deep grooved fingernails then
back on the street again, waves of combustible
breath wheedle, as if marble tongued, rolling,
begging for your spare change, contributions
towards a taste, down the alleys skulk cats
of thin ribs and legs, haunches high, on top
of restaurant garbage spills they flee
the sound of oncoming steps or the sight
of passing shadows, tails whipping
against air grey with sullen bluster
the sky seems to have come low enough to lick
fine moisture washes the surface of your eyes
with circular spots of water lit by
the carnival bumper car spark of the electric
coach passing as you suddenly see
all this loneliness as your own

Standing In Line
Introduction by Jack Hirschman
Jerry D. Miley

STANDING IN LINE
Jerry D. Miley
(1990)

The poems of Jerry Miley are triumphs over the destitution and homelessness into which an indifferent system is daily forcing more and more of its citizens, especially the young. With an unsentimental but incisively feeling pen, Miley tells of the streets, the hungry and the discarded, and of the poorhouse world which has been part of his life.

His poems have a concentrated drift reflecting a world where things become rags and nature endures amid the squalor and poverty of the inescapable Real. Works like "Dim Light", "Memories", "Old Stew Tramp", "Man Nearing Old Age", as well as others in the book, contain such an outcast sincerity that the reader immediately is confronted by an original poetic voice.

It is a book that staggers and stumbles the way men and women do; its sufferings are never whines of self-pity; it is simple and compassionately true to the form of each incident of soul; its song is the song one sings to oneself, but in such a way that all the world can recognize its authenticity.

A poetry of lived life. Just what is necessary!

I'm happy to introduce a new American voice. It will restore one's faith in the poetry of this land, which so often comes from spoiled and privileged imaginations. The forgotten and the trashed and the poor sure need Jerry Miley's ear and pen for the struggles ahead.

Jack Hirschman

DIM LIGHT

In ten minutes
we will stand in line
in ten minutes
our line will move upstairs
in ten minutes
we will have found a place to live
in ten minutes
my exhaustion will lay down
in ten minutes
I will go to sleep
ten minutes

AS WE LEFT THE MISSION

As we left the mission
he spoke to a lone man,
who approaching late middle age
in poverty, hung his head
in loneliness, and spoke low
as if saying:
would we both please go away
and leave him to his
skid row retirement?
other than this
he would not reply;
(we have done something wrong
I think) I had not wanted
to talk to him at all:
we left discussing
his resigned passivity.

OLD STEW TRAMP

He wasn't much -
an old stew tramp

who had eaten stew
for so long

he wore his pants loose
on a hunched lean frame -
he stared through success -
if your failure
got to know him
he'd pull you down
like an old bottle of wine -
a movement of his bowels
when he failed to loop himself
properly,
he never changed
your street material
wasn't good for him -
           he broke it down
he bummed it out -
this is real street,
his indifferent gaze
between pavement and cloud,
he knows he has no place to look.

MEMORIES

I remember memories of awakening
with no memories:
I remember trying to forget:
never do I remember such hopeless
longing to stand up and do something
as in a Skid Row hotel room.
Two years covered up in cold
sheet warmth windows closed,
even the noise was cold,
and steam hissing like a snake
biting itself to sleep by mid-morning,
rattling dreams tossed
themselves a hot plate,
plugging in heat like a stopped-up sink
giving off floor water
when you turned it on:
plaster cracking sound of ancient pipe.
I am moving out of that hotel
to this day
my overlarge heavy white coat
with no buttons

is on my back by 9:30,
and I am waiting forever to go
back to sleep,
because I cannot bare to stay awake
and this is human life
when I am waiting
not to be hungry.

OBSERVATION TWENTY

Two poor ex-working
American men, sitting
with their baggage on a
wooden bench, bored
mission hungry, tired
of starvation five years ago,
when it mattered a little
more than it does now,

A poor man knows
how to get full free -
laughter they will stomach
when it is time to get serious,
because there is nothing else to do
even the sun is out for a chill,
and is shining dully,
there is usually enough sleep;
today, not quite
enough walking

enough food
enough life
gritty noise of crushed stones.

Language isn't graceful
when concrete shows
bird's shadow, where head is
bowed;
and time itself is falling
asleep while two poor
men are lazily awake.

MAN NEARING OLD AGE

Man nearing old age strolling head
bent down, pondering history,
a vague 19th century man
mumbling at two young ladies
in passing, that he wishes
solitude while daylight fades
from his eyes and eccentricity shuts
his purse even to his own hungry mouth.

He is stump walking, feet splayed, mouth open
enough for nose air bushy white aureole of hair,
bearded like a self-appointed saint,
 crossing and recrossing the same path.

CITY'S HOMELESS

Cities of homeless
                    another green shadowed day
paid out like blood
                    on no floor.
City hills flatten eyes
                    wise steps sidle
up to graveled lips
                    crack
                    and fall:
not dancing, dreaming,
                    yearning to sleep
                    with tired ruined flesh,
                    stepping on.

BROKEN MEN

Broken men who no longer care
waiting for their mouths to tear:
playing a game called, 'nothing is fair'.

Broken men who wandering walk;
they don't smile when they talk:

and when they do, its torso stalk.

Broken men, whose steps cry,
slow walking soft knee sigh:
harsh eyes that almost say good-bye.

With each step you do not see,
men sorry to be finally free
give themselves and you, no plea.

SNAKING LINE

A long snaking line, hissing shoe leather,
widening around corners, through shadows,
murals fading like a washed-out eye
as sinewy backs sinuously turn away
from slightly ancient paint.
These men are nearly children, grown lean;
their eyes not questioning age,
nor were they born old, they have
experienced too soon a way of life called
'poverty', where to refuse love
is kind lust, to receive lust, is a perfect
negative goodness.

They have lined up to eat,
and I am waiting with them, waiting to sit down,
hoping no one speaks to me,
staring blandly with a fixed muted
expression, at hallways that reflect
no gleaming merrier like light,
because there is none.

TWO MISSION STORY POEMS

I.

    I'm sitting here, in this mission, near the front, with the
most animalistic Indian, squat, tough, dark, tramped out and
boozy, that you ever saw, and I am hungry, and the religious
fanatic is forty-five minutes into a humdrum, we haven't yet

caught hell, but we're starving heaven out of our personal universe, and I am still hungry - and that drunk brave stands up and says, "Christ is in me!"

And the minister jumps up and this is the most amazing conversion he's ever seen, and one man hems and another one haws, and I do not care in the slightest, I want my dinner, I'm entitled to dinner, and that Indian's standing there, and some man says, "He'll be drunk tomorrow." There is a general nodding of wise old heads. I'm sitting there in all innocence, damning God and devil, for I am hungry.

Wouldn't you know it? Next day he was drunk!

II.

The coffee was always hot, one refill. A plate of cookies, soft, right tasty when dipped in that thick mud cookie sediment at the bottom of the cup. Never any sugar unless you brought your own. Had about ten, fifteen minutes to drink them both off. One morning with all these old men, rubber tramps, hobo half-breeds, young drifters, what have you, I ate too many cookies and this was noticed by a peeved-looking old codger, who looked like a stocky out-of-work-and-not-caring railroad trainyard man. He pushed the tray of cookies towards me with a look saying, "My resignation to you means I don't care. You are going to regret this youngun!" and I do believe he passed it on. To this day, occasionally, someone stares at me, out of the corner of his eye, whenever I eat a sweet.

HOW POOR PEOPLE MEET

Met him at two in the morning
    when he could not sleep,
a warm voice in a chill night
    I thought him simply another creep.

There was no proof, there never is
    when two poor men meet,
there is the question of defeat:
    we are a living, mine and his.

We stood there talking talk
    his views those of a hawk,
I flew very low,
    til I said to him, "Go!"

Simple as that. He has left
      again in poverty. I am bereft:
didn't like him to start off,
         my sense of friendship is this soft.

THE SHIRT

A lonely feeling 6:30 in the evening;
the sun is as it is:
a pair of hands unwashed for two weeks
a crumpled pair of pants near a gutter
where an empty container
with lettering washed off
waits for a sentenced sweeper to
broom up into a dustpan.
A shirt hanging on a steel fence unclaimed;
nonetheless two men stare at you
as you walk by that shirt:
they are light brown men,
the shirt is not theirs
they do not care if you take it,
they stare at you
with faces almost friendly,
you do not dare pick up that shirt,
if you did
would they let you keep it?
It is best if a shirt is left hanging
near two light brown men
who watch you as
(walking by a shirt you almost want)
you see two men staring at you.

THOUGHTS FROM A BROKEN MAN

His room was filthy
and his mind equaled it,
so he told me.

He shook as if wearing his winter

coat in summer
standing on an inner city bridge screaming
out loud at what nobody else could see -

with a voice still retaining vestiges
of education.

Panhandling passers-by for a quarter
to buy a cup of coffee with,
in the rain swaying back and forth
in the cold,
with hands in his pockets, literally begging
for change;
he told me several times that his father
who hated him
was an ex-shipping magnate who lost everything
when he, the son, was only seven years old:

Now his son was left to wander the streets
after two years of mental hospitalization
for schizophrenia, or maybe he was lying
and the Oregon labor unions got to him
because he eloquently, profanely seemed to
know a lot about Oregon labor unions, besides
their 'sucking eggs', as he put it;
in derision of their policies:
maybe they did it to him.

WHILE IT IS WARM

While it is warm, here
I will write a drop-in story.
An old mexican in used clothes
sits in an over-stuffed donated
easy chair reading the paper,
while outside the second story
picture windows, it is dark:
he has written to his ex-wife
in her new home, honoring
their life together,
from a free shelter he pays for
by being laconic and tough,
this is his tramp world,

he is proud to be called this
in near old age,
walking down the street
scratching his stretched-out
armpits, while my accidental eye
follows him away from his usual
sleep place, the shelter where
I am waiting to be let up for a
foreshortened night's sleep.
Bad night for a quiet man
who sits in an easy chair
reading a newspaper.

WALKED OUT

Walked out of an
over-populated door -

past a 'he's a bum,
low on luck'
sleeping in scuffy
jeans, near to
a 7:30 locked store
door, below the picture
window loaded with cameras,
stereos, watches, shirts
overshadowing
this one man's hell
on cement earth.

SHE KNEW BETTER
Wendy-o Matik
(1991)

FOR WHAT LITTLE IT'S WORTH TO YOU

If it makes you feel any better,
   I'll take the blame
   I'll be happy to pardon your forgiveness
   relieve you of your responsibility
If it makes you feel any better,
   beat the crap out of me
   teach me a lesson I'll never forget
   remind me what a coward I am
The fear that runs your life ragged with disappointment
   tie me to the friggin' cross
   If it'll make you feel better,
   Why not.
   And while you're at it,
   pointing out all my other
   disgusting flaws and inconsistencies,
Lay into me one last good blow
   for the wicked times to come
One final painful gut-wrenching
   twist of the blade
   for the purging of one's own Hell on Earth.
It shouldn't be too difficult
   you've gotten so good at it by now
And maybe it'll make you feel
   just a little bit better
   maybe you'll even smile inside
   pat yourself on the back old man
   and then pass me that ice pack.

HIDING THE PASSION
dedicated to Ali

I remember her fantasy about
  wanting to end it all under water
  the both of them
  poisoned by love, two dead souls
  like two dead weights
  on the bottom of the sea
  Alone together at last
  swollen sunken heartship
  The perfect love tragedy, I thought.

I recall her craving
  to sleep with two men
  Sandwich of love, as they say.
  It was a time of chance and
  exploring herself,
  Sex sort of sucked her in
  like a magnet and she let loose.
  I would be out there if the tides washed her
  too far out, I had promised.

I can remember her crazy reality
  giving without taking
  (taking without asking)
  A heart set on love and eternity
  A spirit bound to find a few of the
  answers to the Ways of the World.
  Ever patient and trusting
  And the only person I know on this planet
  who could pull off being
  completely hopeless and perfectly together.

I'll never forget the times
  we burst into laughter
  youthful giggling, non-stop
  unconscious to time and troubles
  our cries silenced by our laughing
  We'd make a pact one day
  to let them both out.
  We'd come too far
  to hide the passion between us.

CRACK-CHILD

It never occurred to her
  what was struggling underneath the pillow
  that she hadn't slept in four days
or that she had a lot of explaining to do
  once the cops got here
  because the body
  limp-like at her feet
  wasn't cryin' no more.

She had begged for silence

like a preacher hails the heavens

Would a judge and jury understand her?
Would her own mama forgive her?

It never occurred to her
that night,
    there was no real escape
    that her baby was like some kind of
        bad crack deal with the government welfare system.

It never occurred to her
    that her baby was only cryin'
        as hard as she had always wanted to cry out
        but didn't let herself.

I don't think I really understood her story either
except that welfare never came
    she just wanted the pain to go away
    and she didn't know who to ask for help.

EVER THOUGHT ABOUT IT

What happens,
    when the wads of garbage that you pass on the highway
    begin to look like severed body parts
    and human appendages?
you know you're losing it

What happens
    when your close friends begin to resemble
    a dumping ground for garbage, a human wasteland?
nobody said it would be like this

What happens
    when what is,   isn't
    what was,   wasn't
    what could have been,   can never be?
what does it all mean?
what will happen to us?

Social Insignificance: reads the newspaper headline
                            cries the atheist

       chuckles the president

The drum beats like the pounding in my head
the tremors encasing my shallow existence
and I wondered
 what ever happened
 to the sandbag full of dreams?
and why do I always feel so manipulated
 by the circumstances beyond my control?

Maybe there's someone who can tell me

What happens
 to the ugly ones,
 girls like me.

SHE SAYS
dedicated to E.N.

she says she doesn't want to live anymore
she says she doesn't want to see me
And my words
 roll off her back
 dissipating into an airless room
 a disconnected phone
 like a balloon you let go to the sky
    as an offering to the gods

I have been here before
pounding on the same door
that never answers you back
The times that have been most
 difficult to breathe
An effortless world of pain
 swallows up the weak and fragile

And I felt something die inside me too
spitting up teeth and blood
a battle I could never win
And it didn't matter
 how many arms and hands
 that tried to reach out
I had already long forgotten

how to accept them
how to shut people out of my misery
She lies silent
       hollow
       numb
at a dead end street
The drum beats like the poundings in my heart
and I can't let go
   all those years
I told her I'd rather spend a lifetime in hell with her
  than spend it on earth without her
I told her
  "whatever doesn't kill you
  only makes you stronger" in the end
and the receiver went dead.

SATISFACTION

she belly flopped
  on a sheet of glass
and felt better.
One usually does
  when love takes a
  backdoor hike
  with little remorse.

Life flowed through her
  like a polluted river
cancerous
disease-ridden
acidic
  with disregard to their warnings
  she went ahead and dove in
It made little difference
Love had already swept her
  under the rug
  and called her a whore.

That night,
  the streets were empty.
She barricaded herself in her bedroom
but the moon burned through
  the curtains like hot wax

She stared at her homemade tattoos
and wondered why all the male poets
  from the last century
  had never made her feel anything
and how tired she'd become
  of reading more poems about men
  who couldn't get laid

And it was this night
  that she wrote about the fire burning inside all women
  a poem created out of blood and saliva and sweat
  a poem shaking its fists at the world, screaming in outrage
  a poem wet with salty tears

an evil witches brew, seething and overflowing
about the longing, being trapped in this body
a poem, loaded and cocked, dangerous and unpredictable
a poem demanding equality and respect

And after days
of agonizing over each word
                    each sound
she closed her eyes
  and felt satisfied
  that she'd finally written something
  that you don't have to have a penis to relate to.

HE SCARES ME

He scares me.
I can't look into my brother's eyes
the black empty holes
holding in the truth
that my brother was part of
  a scientific experiment
  backed by the government
  some kind of mind control
  a chemical processed in their food
  which would release a stimulant
  that taps into unleashed human aggression
They call the experiment: war
the vietnam war
a whole generation of obedient boys

easily manipulated by their lies
turned into savages
a psychological warfare

And it's those black empty holes
  like minefields
  trapping his violent tendencies
          his hatred of women
a sickness that makes him hate himself
and anyone else who gets too close.

Those bottomless black holes
  eaten away by too many drugs and alcohol
  burned open by denial
the metal plate in his head where he was shot
he fights the battle in his mind
losing to paranoia and isolation
He scares me.

I haven't seen him for five years
he only calls between 12 a.m. and 8 a.m.
  and everything he says scares me.
I think he's losing it
I mean, really losing it.
The voice on the other end—scares me

He says he knows where I live—it scares me
Even his laugh scares me.

He calls to get our dad's number,
  but that number was changed
  when he threatened them
  one too many times.
He calls asking for his ex-wife's number,
  but there's a protective order
  on her house and children.
And I can't give him what he wants
    I can't stop his war
    I can't give him peace.
He keeps finding me
tracing my number from town to town
always taking from me
        taking my emotions
always stealing from me
        stealing my kindness
He's my brother

so I'm supposed to be giving
but when will he stop taking?

How do I tell my brother
   that the war has only just begun for him
   that there was no real escape for any of us,
   and I love him
   and I care about him
   and I need him to leave
                   leave me
                   leave me alone.

COLD CHILL

a cold chill ran up the back of her spine
could she ever forget?
he stalked her like a shadow
glancing over her shoulder
she ran
slipping, skidding forward
skinned knees, falling forward
scrambling to her feet again
         (if she were a man
            she would have stood up to him)
running harder
no time to breathe
the chase had sucked her in
she didn't dare look back.
This time,
   it didn't matter what she was running from
   her own shadow
   fear
   a man
because this time
She could never stop.

In a world of disenchantment
a body
stumbles in the darkness
cornered by fear
she's forgotten how to sleep
she's lost her will to face reality

and no one can save her from herself.

WHAT LITTLE I HAD LEFT

I scoped out a place to sit
   somewhere on the outskirts of people
   or dogs or cars
   or you
   somewhere at the edge of existence
                  a nowhere spot
                  a non-space
   somewhere too far to make eye contact
   or recognize anyone
   or to feel hopeful
   too distant to force a smile
                  or gesture a 'hello'

The pain of solitude
   sort of sucked me in
   like a bad dream that you never wake up from
   no matter how loud you scream.

I fell back in an uneasy slump
thinking more about what I had let happen
and less about what lie ahead
caught up in the emotion of it all
and finding it easier to put the rationale to rest

I swallowed a lost strand of your angel fine hair
taking in
what little I had left
while knowing in my heart
that I wanted more of you.

It took all that I have inside me to tell you this.

LEFT INSIDE

the sex
spelled out

on her lips
forced me to my knees
as only a woman can
fall downwards
arms that forget to reach out
eyes like trenches
swollen and sunken
she had purged herself of a grief
   measured only by dark circles and creases,

Love parked herself on a curb
   freshly dyed hair and nails to match
   aerosol tickled her nose.
She let them go
the men in her life
the ones who had taken from her
every bit of self-worth left inside.
She let their pain and empty words
   seep down her thigh.

It was just another day,
In a lifetime
   of selling one's self short
   of dreams that never come true
Inside a heartfelt woman
                     dying
                     alone

SHE MOVES ME

It must be something like
the tingling in the finger
on the trigger

Or that quivering
of a hungry child's lips
waiting to be fed

It's just gotta be like
the Earth and the Moon
passing one another in orbit
catching but small
glimpses of the Universe

It must be like an unleashed scream
in a silent cathedral
Holy-Jesus-Fucking-Mary

She holds the reigns
    of her life
She lets the dead weight
    roll off her back
She moves
            unmatched
            unscathed
she stuns me
  like gravity and atmosphere
  from the tenth floor
  She meets the pavement
  and stands tall

Cat's eyes on fire
She's got lightening
shoved in her back pocket-
And nobody but the devil and the deep blue sea
can sink this woman
cause that's
how   she moves me.

PARADOX

I believe that
if men could design women
into functional extensions
of an ideal playmate
Women would be like video games
robot-like toys
fully animated and programmed
    and don't forget the mute button
We would play music
    instead of speak
We would cook and clean
    instead of complaining
    about how dirty the house is
We would always have orgasms
    instead of lying about them.

They would stop treating us
  like their mothers
  and make commitments
  and appreciate us.

We would program
irresistible hockey games
  challenging video simulators
  digital everything
They would push all the right buttons
Our bodies
sophisticated by technology
for men.

The heterosexual paradox
is not a simple one.
I will always feel more
connected with women
Men have continually
alienated and frightened me
I have no language
to converse equally with men
They cannot understand me.

I am silent
I cook meals silently
And beneath the silence
  you can hear me
  whisper poetry
  through telephone airwaves
  to lonely women at the other end
  and we celebrate
  in our connectedness and love for one another
  our secret affairs
Beneath the silence
  I hear others tell similar
   stories of dissatisfaction and fear
  eyes that look into your soul
  bodies that brush up against each other
   in comfort

She feels hunted down
She is on the defense
They speak the latest video lingo
She is silent
She is a goal

penetrated by angry missiles.
She is somebody's war toy.

FRAGMENTED WOMEN

It was like giving birth
   to a death
an unconscious evil
bottled up inside her
in a place where it hurt to laugh or
                        to feel anything or
                        to tell anyone
She found herself at the same dead end
restless and uncreative
serving time
   at someone else's request

An abandoned outpost of some kind
her mind ticking away
   like a rattlesnake in the desert
dust heavy on her face

"50 now, 50 later"
he meant trouble
there are places
   where 911 doesn't mean shit
   where evidence goes up in flames
   and the case starts to smell real bad.

She feels like she's always running
   because the gunshots keep getting louder
   in her neighborhood
   because friends are dropping out of school
   and working at pizza joints
   because she's getting more and more behind
   all the time
And there's just not enough to keep her afloat.

She sips on another beer
thinking she never used to drink alone
she keeps the shades down
   and the sun out
and is convinced that

happiness is an illusion

she can't tell the difference
   between fact and fiction
what can she believe in anymore?

"Yer on!"
she bet him her last five
"5 now, 5 later"
a smile rose on her face
   like a wild card
she knew she'd already won
   since he was just another born loser
   in her book
Winning, that's what it was all about for him,
she knew better.

So she sat around
   watching tv
   while American pesticides
   sterilized another generation of field workers
So she sat around
   writing poetry
   while the CIA played big-in-the-pants
   with their covert wars
"Checkmate"
she hates chess
       games in general for that matter
So she sat around
   til her ass felt numb
   til she stopped answering the phone
and she thought about the women
   who held onto their men
   by having babies,
because while their men
had room for creative freedom
the women still regret
   not learning an instrument
   and taking control of their lives
   still waiting around for Mr. Right
   to bring meaning to their lives
Then the baby came
filling the void when he would leave.

She wondered when it would be their turn

to express themselves
all those women
all that bottled up love and rage
she understood why they did what they did.

But it still makes her cry
   knowing that she's missing out.
Because how long is it gonna take
   before we get it together?
How long is it gonna take
   before we put the judgments to rest
   and make a dent in our own history?

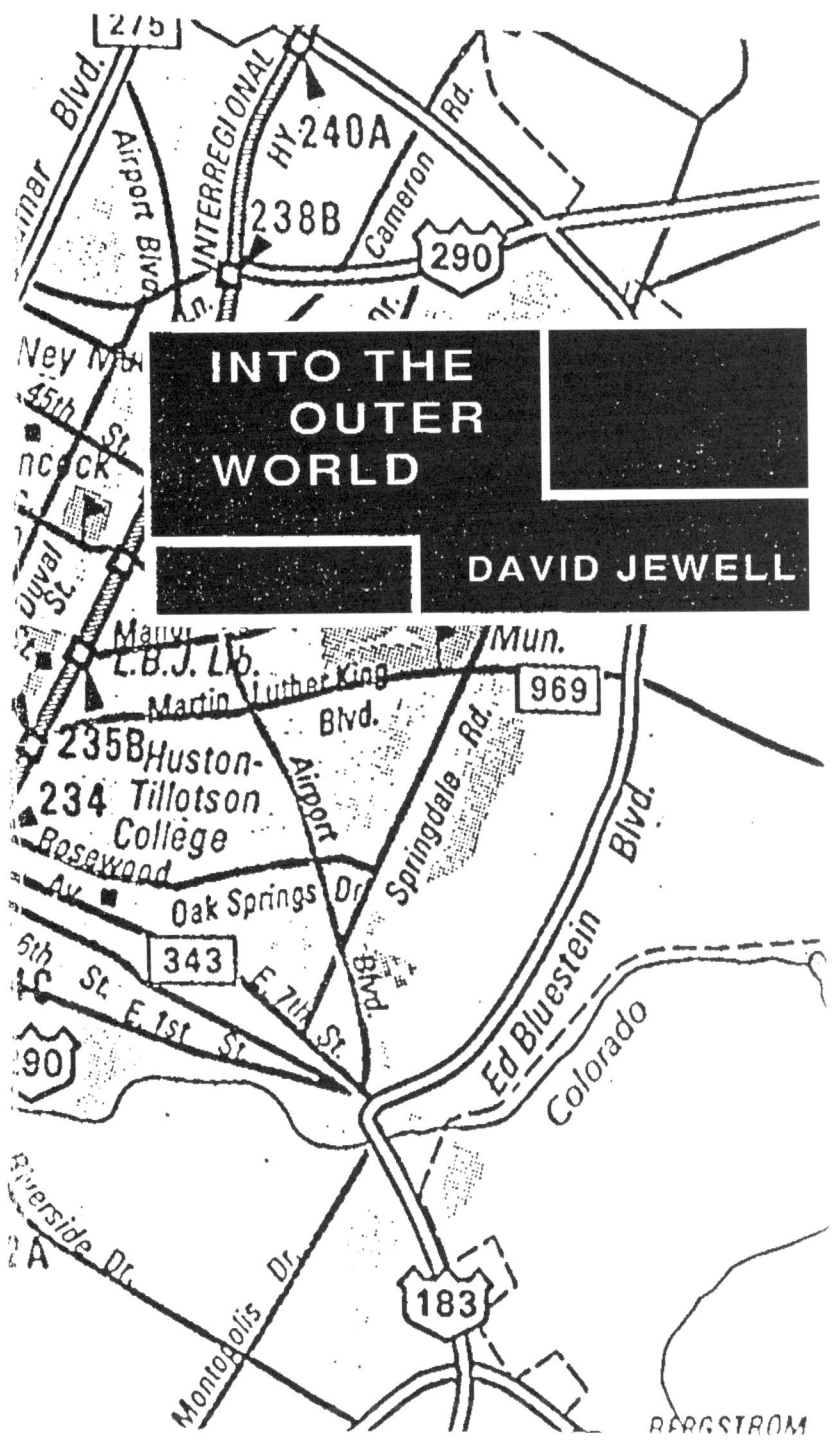

INTO THE OUTER WORLD

DAVID JEWELL

INTO THE OUTER WORLD
David Jewell
(1990)

into the outer world
into the other world

where backbone is guide
where waves begin & break

where you are refracted
like moonlight on lake

where desire is a panther
w/ patience wearing thin

a motor boat to oblivion
where reality tends to bend

& you find yrself stranded
among diamonds
w/ no real cash to spend

in a foreign country
ordering coffee
all day long
reading the map
of yr hand like a fated
moment.

He could not believe she was gone.
No matter what she did to prove it to him.
He thought if he let himself believe it he would die
instantly. He didn't know who was moving
his body around everyday—but it
wasn't him.

He didn't know where he was.
Someplace in the ocean
without a map.

Someplace where there were
no walls or sidewalks.

Birds fly free
out of mouth
build nests
in heart
leap in mind
through the air
make horrible
chirping racket
in brain
remind you
of lost lover's name
over and over and over
you see the feathered beasts
you leap at them to grab them
they swim away through the air

dive like bombers
through your whole sense of balance
& every day non-stop the same question
& the same answer
& the same body to move around in

Machine behind eyes cranking visions
(brain screen gone haywire)

the hopelessness of controlling another's behavior
(the difficulty of controlling self)

ricochet of time
(bullwhip crack regret stinging nerves)

two people on boat in stormy sea
(one person jumps off what do you have)

as much water outside as there are tears inside
(struggling swimmer)

bobbing up for third time
(hands reach out to grasp)

no longer there

fist of innocence tongue of dread
yesterday has so many apologies
tomorrow so many excuses

I've seen people sitting in their apartments
clutching raw meat in their hands
tearing at it like wild dogs

the logic of emotion
like nuclear test sites

what is really said under all the words
is I love you
what do you expect from me
nature hates this vacuum cleaner

victims are experts at lacerating themselves
so all their expectations will come true
they can't bear the unknown

what is really said under all the words is
touch me   hold me gently

let this moment come alive
let the future stay outside
let the past evaporate & die

what is really said under all the words is
come on now...

I walk along the frozen shadow
(I am the shadow) I walk in the shade
(on the shady side)
I keep my curtains closed
I glance behind me

I go for a ride   (a drive)
I walk all over town   (I drive all over town)

I am looking for something

something that is gone that used to be
a hand some skin those eyes that touch that
sound of voice that way of moving
those secret syllables

 what is it now
the other bucket seat empty
the plans of nowhere nothing no one
don't know how can't remember how
why when you were gone...

The closet of the place I moved out of was so empty
you could fall through another dimension there and
I did as I left and walked out of that closet so empty
I barely had the hands to carry it all and I love it
in a way—this giddy freedom—and I curse it like a dog
at my heels barking in its pip-squeak voice.

too much sad smile I can't see through the veil of
this heartache some frenzy below the surface
boiling wants release and wants connection

your eyes a memory
I keep hoping to be reminded by your eyes
there in front of me I can talk to

before ice grows on my tongue
before bats hide in the cave of my chest
before chains bite into flesh & I see that face
in front of me everyday it isn't there...

my pillow cries your name
asking for your velvet cheek
asking for your fragrance.

winter night oblivion
as they are all oblivious
as winter is always like that

as the days
having so much less light in them
fade fast

at the same time sluggish
it's that lack of heat
all those closed windows

all those strange heaters
with what they do to the air
all those clothes you wear

that make things seem so heavy.

The channel splashes another reality on my optic
nerves
& my emotions slither away like so many lost
detectives.

Strapped behind the barbed wire of commercials,
my mind wanders to another room where she used
to be bathing, calling my name from time to time
so I would visit.

But there is only silence there now & the hollow drip
from the faucet. I can not sustain any thought—
the memory devours me like another hungry
panther feeding on the panther that devoured me
before.

He wanted to talk to her even though he had
nothing coherent to say. He wanted to walk into
a room & stand in front of her & dance like a
chimpanzee. Grunt, moan, stomp his feet,
pound his chest, screech, roll on the floor.
He thought this would be the only way to
communicate with her, the only way to show her
how he felt. He thought by doing this he could
save them both hours   of   abstract
conversation.

my love is a python wrapped around your feet
you struggle

my love becomes a bird
you reach into the air
I land on your finger

you close your fist
my love becomes a big bear with claws and teeth
you're scared

my love becomes a fish flopping out of water
you throw me in the bath tub
my love becomes a dragon

you lock me in a cave
my love becomes smoke and leaks out of the
door
your eyes water you can't breathe you plead

my love turns into a human being
& I hold you in my arms
& you hold me.

stoplight skull fracture
in the middle of the night
w/ the beast pouring through you

while the energy is going
& the momentum is there
& the alcohol demands indifference...

but very few people actually stop
at stoplights
they stop their cars
but their engines their bodies their minds
keep churning   to the rhythm of the radio
or something lighter   or darker
or some imaginary conversation
or fantasy of heat...

to get moving   to be in motion
instead of just sitting there
when the rhythm is inside you
& the night is hot
w/ some vibes from a distant planet
so everything is slanted
a couple of degrees...

aware that this is a planet among many
w/ a slightly better health plan than most
but no less outrageous for that.

The guilt monsters went out for drinks

they were hailing cabs

they were stepping out

they were playing snare drums on stage

they were throwing cups of ice

over their shoulders indiscriminately

the guilt monsters were renting rooms

fishing from their balconies

making prank phone calls

jumping in the fountain

the guilt monsters were swinging from the elevator cables

they were shoplifting in the gift shop

they were throwing spare change on the railroad tracks

and waking people up.

sundown city
shatter vision
night like a shower
of stars keep falling
you feel everyone

& your body just a creature
absorbing the universe
feels the light
on its skin
    and sheds its connection
    to time.

I've forgotten everything
tongue w/o a sound
bankruptcy of emotion
leaving dull pain
search among women
for tender touch
fruit of love
disconnected now
phone off hook
like once flowers
now thorns
beauty and pain
unbearable
saw winter

thought relief
watched flowers die
slow
back to ground
and left this desert
where the wind is like a razor now.

sleepy dawn surrender
hands hiding behind yr eyes
pulling the curtains of consciousness closed
filtering all the light
leaving only the subtleties & dreams
& shadows
like loose connections
that vanish
in the air.

Birds outside
chirping like the world's perfect—
cars drive by.

Life is not the problem
the problem is how to live it.

Quite honestly I don't know what to do—
I need to breathe fresh air.

DRUGS
Jennifer Joseph
(1989)

WET SHEETS

He told her to wait in the car, he'd be right back. She drew designs on the fogged-up inside windows, and listened to the music in her head. The concert had been worth the long drive in the middle of winter. Five hours across Ohio, the last one lost outside of Columbus.

He came back to the car, his friend with him. The two boys got in the car: John in the front seat next to the girl, his friend climbed in the back. John opened the glove compartment and started counting sheets of paper.

"They're still wet," he said. "That's how fresh they are."

"If they're still wet you better not touch them," the girl said. "You'll be up all night anyway, it's gonna be hours before we come down, and you're gonna end up staying awake until tomorrow."

"Yeah, cool, right on," the guy in the back seat mumbled, handing a big wad of bills to John. "You might want to count it but it's all there."

John thumbed quickly through the cash. "Yes, yes indeed," he said. "Here you go. This is for twenty, right?"

"Yeah, cool, thanks... are you guys finishing the tour?"

"I guess we're going to a few more shows," the girl said. "See you tomorrow night in Indianapolis."

FEDERAL EXPRESS

The doorbell rang.

"I hope it's the Federal Express guy. I've been waiting for Mike to send me this package from Ohio. I mean, he said he would send it as soon as I left, and it's already been a week."

"Hey Tom, it's the Federal Express guy. And guess what? The package is for you."

"Cool. This must be the three thousand dollars I've been waiting for." He opened the package and pulled out an envelope that was inside the mailer. It wasn't sealed. Empty.

"What?!" he said. "Whoa, something is very wrong here. Mind if I call Ohio?"

"No. Go right ahead. Damn, that's weird."

Tom hung up the phone. "Shit. Fuck. Piss. Damn." He was visibly upset. "That asshole... how could he? I mean he's like my best friend, but... Jesus Christ!"

"What happened?"

"Seems that the Federal Express guy came to his house to pick it up before Mike had a chance to put the cash in an envelope so the guy like stood there watching him while Mike put the money in the... you know as soon as he got into that truck, he helped himself to the cash - my money. Shit, man, someone's gonna have to pay for this. This is totally fucked up."

"So is Mike gonna have to make it up to you? I mean I guess it's his responsibility. What a stupid fuckin' thing to do. I can't fuckin' believe that."

"No shit. Yeah, it's Mike's problem now."

"How's he gonna get that kind of money together?"

"I dunno. But he'll have to figure something out. Bummer."

"Yeah. Bummer."

LOU REED

"Let's get some hash," she said, as they walked toward the Piazza.

"Maybe," he replied. "It might be hard to find. Wait here."

He deposited her at a sidewalk café. "I'll be right back." He crossed the piazza and disappeared down a narrow side street.

A waiter brought her a beer. She drank her Peroni alone and understood why the Italians were famous for wine and not beer. She stared at the label, avoiding eye contact with other people. The last time she waited for someone at this café, a drunken Turkish guy wouldn't leave her alone.

Her friend returned and said, "It's not possible. All they have in this neighborhood is Lou Reed. We have to go to Piazza Navona to get hash." He drank her beer.

"What do you mean they only have Lou Reed?"

He shrugged. "You know, Lou Reed."

"What does Lou Reed have to do with anything?"

He looked at her like she was a stupid American.

BALLOONS

They wandered down Ninth Avenue looking for the apartment door number.

"I think this is it," she said. "Look at the balloons by the mailbox here. Ho-ho, pretty funny."

"No kidding."

Opening the door, they heard the unmistakable sound of a nitrous party. The sound of nitrous coming out of a tank was loud going into the balloons. The laughter and voices were almost as loud as the shush of gas rushing out of the tank. These parties are great, she thought, even if the burn-out level is enormous. I like being burned-out. All this awareness is killing me.

She walked into the room where the tank was parked. The floor was littered with bodies. Enormous balloons replaced people's faces. Everyone looked vaguely familiar. Someone announced, "The tank's empty!" and a big moan went up as people clamored for more.

More, more, there's never enough. The only enough is too much. It was only how much you could get without getting too much, that was the key to the whole process.

A voice said, "No, man, it's only frozen on the bottom. Here, check it out. If you tilt it sideways, y'see, like this ... right, you got it, it helps the gas move around, right, there ya go, y'see there's plenty left."

Great. She kind of fell in line, even though it wasn't really a line. There was a definite order to how long people had been waiting to fill their balloons, and the people who had been waiting the longest made that very clear. She filled her balloon, and pushed her way toward the hallway past a guy who spilled vodka on her sleeve. She spotted the friends she had come to the party with, and asked if they wanted some nitrous.

"Nah, I did that stuff a lot in high school, and now it just gives me headaches."

"Oh. That's too bad." She wrapped her lips around the mouth of the balloon and breathed in slowly. She inhaled as slowly as she could and kept the gas in her lungs as long as possible. Her ears rang with wave patterns, ordered yet unattached to anything. She saw people's mouths moving as they spoke to her, but all she could do was laugh. Her mind was perfectly clear.

"I'm glad I'm driving home from this party," her square friend said. All she could do was laugh harder.

It's always the same, she thought, it's always the same.

FIRST CHAPTER

"It was amazing," he said. "I read the first chapter of this story I had written, and the professor stopped and came over and gave me a kiss, and told me that she thought I was one of the best students she had ever had. She said if I ever wanted to get published, she would help me."

"Wow. You're taking that class at Berkeley? So why don't you take her up on the offer? You can't go on doing what you do now forever. I mean, if she really thinks you're that good, why don't you just go for it? What have you got to lose?"

"It's not that I have anything to lose. But what's the point? I could never make as much money writing as I do now."

"How can you be so sure? All the talent in the world is nothing without manifestations. One of these days you're gonna have to make a choice."

"Yeah, well, in the meantime, I'm going to Asia and spending some of this money on myself before I have to give it all to a lawyer to get me out of jail. I'll figure out what I'm gonna to do next when I get back."

LUCIANO

The phone rang.

"Hello, Jen? This is Luciano. I'm back from New York and wanted to call. Don't worry about the money, that's not why I called. Of course, if you could get it to me by Monday, that'd be cool, because I'm going up North again and stuff, but whatever... So, let me tell you about New York. I had a great time there this time. When I get back from Thailand, that's definitely where I'm moving to. Like, I think I've done San Francisco. I've lived here for a while and there's just not that much going on. But wow, New York was really something else this time. It was wild. You could imagine. You know the whole thing. Clubs, serious restaurants. Stayed in this really nice hotel. I'm going to get my own apartment in Manhattan when I get back though...

"But man, it was nuts. Like you know I haven't done any of the heavy stuff in like three years. But this time in New York I did it every day for a week. It was nuts.... No, I didn't shoot it. We did lines. But shit man like these people we got it from in the East Village, like the first coupla times I got it from them it wasn't as good as the last time, the last weekend I was there, and wooo-eee, were we ill... like really out of it, y'know? I was with this really young 18-year-old girl and she could barely handle it... we went to see "Sid & Nancy" and man it was just like that... Sitting there on the hotel bed with the t.v. on, dropping cigarette ashes all over the goddam bed... Man, I'll never forget walking out of that movie theater on the West Side, and like walking across

Central Park at one in the morning all fucked up y'know, and this enormous fuckin rat ran across my foot... I couldn't believe it... right across my foot... New York's just like that... I can't wait to go back...

"It's weird though. Since I've been back on the West Coast, like last week, I started having trouble seeing out of my left eye. Like, I can't see at all, but whatever... I went to see this eye doctor and he said I might need laser surgery but we'll see about that... I mean it's already costing me a fortune just to see the guy, he's a specialist, y'know? So, anyway, I'm too young to worry about my health, I'm only twenty-nine after all... so... anyway, if you could get me that money over the weekend that'd be cool, because what with this doctor shit and going up North and everything, it'd be a good thing. Okay, glad everything's cool with you. I'll see you on Saturday. Bye."

THIS IS FOR

This is for the girl who spent hours wandering around the parking lot looking for her friends and the car after a particularly dosed-out show

This is for H., who ate an ounce of mushrooms and went to the hospital after he chewed up his fingers till they were bloody.

This is for L., who shared a lot of ecstasy one New Year's Eve, and lost it completely two weeks later. Seventy-two hours.

This is for M., who sat in a small room tripping all night after dosing at two in the morning, and called her mother in Oklahoma the next day to tell her about Jimi Hendrix.

This is for R., who broke both ankles jumping out a second story window in the Haight, in a fit of cocaine paranoia. The doorbell rang and he was sure it was the Feds. It was only the mailman.

This is for B.T., who spent years in San Quentin for trying to smuggle 25,000 hits of acid out of the country, and took care of nasty little teenagers in the Haight when he got out. Last word was that he blew his leg off robbing banks in the Midwest to support his habit.

This is for J., who was in jail in Jersey, and for J., who was in jail in Ohio, and for E., who is in jail in Texas.

This is for those who've reached escape velocity, broken free from the gravitational pull, and never regretted it for a single moment.

BEAUTY AND SADNESS

We put this piece of paper on our tongues
and dissolve into endless volumes of vivid stories untold
Our tongues have frozen
we cannot speak
yet the words are infinite
    raining like rubber bullets
    bouncing off profound sounds
laughter fills our throats
    spreading smiles across our dilated eyes
How can we describe the sixth most sacred sense?

Perhaps it will always be a personal secret
    the monstrosity of mystery
    beauty and sadness
    understanding and abandonment
where does the brick end and the mortar begin?
where does the mortality begin?
I developed a taste for
instant imitation immortality
at a very young age
and I just want to tell you
we will never be the same
I just want to tell you
we can never be the same

NINE SEVEN SIX

"Susan's working at a phone sex fantasy place to support her habit. You know, one of those 976 numbers. It was the only job she could find after she got fired from the last one for stealing books and reselling them."

Peter looked serious. He continued, "She says that most of the men who call there want her to pretend that she's their girlfriend. They want her to pretend she's strapping on a dildo and fucking them up the butt."

"Is that what men fantasize about?" I asked.

"That's what she said," he replied.

"What does Susan fantasize about?"

"Free heroin," he said.

NIGHT IS COLDER THAN AUTUMN

Jerry D. Miley

NIGHT IS COLDER THAN AUTUMN
Jerry D. Miley
(1991)

DISILLUSION

Disillusion is a cold feeling
during a food line.
Think of chill eyes staring
you down like a sun
that has been going down
for a million years,
and has chosen this moment
to collapse completely
all over you, leaving nothing.
And when these eyes look up
in darkness, where a patina
of red flows in fiery
instability, feel every
morning of summer,
like a last day.

PICTURE

Allowing a dream to remain awake:
I slept until night closed blue
this air of thought;
until I expelled night
from my eyes, and sought
for day to begin with vision
lighter than a star.
Dreams no longer cloud my eyes.
Thought is a wisp of a symbol.
Feeling wind clear day, I
consider these faint blue
beginnings of first night.

NIGHT IS COLDER THAN AUTUMN

Night is colder than autumn
until morning,
where there is no warmth:
another day of walking
as cars pass.

This day is no warmer than summer.
I walk up another freeway:
blasted mountain road wending
through a maze of red ribboned ore
shining, rock smashed bone,
ancient burial mounds
of warfare, lost life,
or circular grains of sunlight's travel.
Night is colder than autumn:
this day is no warmer than summer:
arrowhead flaked roadside chips
of boulder-strewn forest,
or autumn's mountain top chill-formed mist.

CHECKERED SUITCOAT

Wearing his checkered suitcoat
in third mission pew,
he smiles to himself
like a pretty man with
a red face weathered
by a storm of roaring poverty
flooding his veins over
the rock of his chest
smooth with this thunderous flesh.
Did the hot summer of his room
dry him out of his mind?
And where did it winter
when he was not this frozen?
Night is outside a mission window
where I glance upon entering.
These are thoughts from a poet
of him. As I sit down, he
is smiling to himself, again
with sadness near the wrinkles
of his mouth.

THE IRISH TENOR

The Irish tenor who drank too much
lifts his voice like a half-full glass
and downs noise with a smile between
contempt and satisfaction
with a smirk of bliss on his face.
If only his mirror image
could see the joke he wants to break open
like every bottle with a sour twist.
If only he could pour his voice forth
into all the corners of this auditorium!

Where sleepy-eyed street people
are tuned awake, prior to a water and bean soup,
raising them up, on a high note of hunger.

NOBODY WANTS TO REMEMBER THE STREET

Nobody wants to remember the street
every cripple needs two feet:

I'll tell you why: they get old here,
living in such low-rent fear.

Take 'Wooden Grin' for all he's got,
leave him just an old stew pot;

Once belonged to 'Henry Leg'
thieving took him down a peg;

She had both legs, arms to boot,
like men huge and hirsute;

Lived two rooms down from 'Limp' himself,
still alive tho' in poor health.

Nobody wants to remember the street,
where men like these are easy to greet;

And where can humanity care for these,
whose bitter lives say "No" like "Please"?

I insist their human state
can place itself among what's great:

And what are you to lower them,
some kind of glinting precious gem

you've stolen from a hock shop near,
where these men are allowed free beer?

Nobody wants to remember the street,
shining like an old pants seat;

unencrusted hat tilted wind sideways,
man below it lost in a daze.

Shirt buttoned against winter night,
nude man near it must be tight:

I saw a man smashing bricks,
he yelled out, "I hate them ticks!"

Some guy answered, "Check your face,
and put them bricks in your place."

A wasted-looking man walked long
strides singing a shrill street song,

across from where two men spoke
of what it means to go for broke,

and stand still upon pavement's gray
because there is no work today.

Plenty of old clothes and food,
enough to make a man feel stewed.

THE CHILD STAR

The child star sat in the third mission row,
straw haired, waiting for his evening meal,
silent as wind against a thick window,
bagging his clothes with clenching fingers,
raw, with a sunburnt appearance,

this person, who had spent half a homeless life
searching for shelter, and these past few months
had room to himself.
He kept quiet there, too,
like a jewel box in a pawn shop window
that had once belonged to (so it was said)
an aged Hollywood queen.
This box had been in a small shop window
for some three years.
It was like a child star.
He thought so to himself
with a face rough with handsome thought:
knowing a few things about pretty objects
he kept to his own language about them
and said nothing.

WHO IS PUTTING HER UP TO THIS?

Who is putting her up to this
in a Tenderloin corner neighborhood store?
And she is reaching for
an open container of hair brushes
with a toothy grin,
like the tow haired little man
stuffing gloves down his pants
and she is looking beyond him, too.
The clerk at the register, staring at
these rare smiling customers to be:
and the boy is thinking about winter
and evening, and the woman exists
as a form of false radiance
under a hundred watt bulb, and her wrist
is turning itself flat and straight
as an ironing board, and the kid has hidden
a pair of stolen gloves completely away
by now, and numbers register on the face
of the man behind the counter,
and he is beginning to feel pressed
against them.

CRAZY

She is a crazy woman
knowing her mouth is open
like a business, giving herself
a bad name, forgotten,
a management new personality,
foreclosing on previous renters,
she bought them out for three months,
she knows she is waiting inside
with open purse counting coins
with mouth closed,
until an old personality opens
her mouth for a business.
She is a crazy woman
in the penury of her pittance,
in the reign of her riches.

HOW OFTEN

How often winter storms freeze themselves
into a blue pattern over a barren mountain!
Seen from an urban jungle, where twisted shapes
of summer burst forth in quick motion,
does the spirit of a wind lash onto summer's last leaf?

There should be more than mere poverty of a stricken human
    being here,
there should be more than a tumor-like growth near a
    poor man's mouth
in a time of sickness with a demand for air, and more air.

There should be more than poetic language:

The sun is going down over a cold landscape:
its red colorations contrasting with shivering human flesh,
yet the chill of this flesh is reddened with the color of blood
    by cold
on its surface
during the darkness of late evening.
And when morning brings forth its warmth
does not its light brown shade have a darkness in it?

HOPPING A BOXCAR

Hopping a boxcar with two American army privates, late at night;
one huge American Negro, one huge American white,
neither of whom could open a sliding boxcar door;
we leaned against that dark rust red boxcar on its siding,
coupled with freight pointing at a main railway line,
and decided, like elusive peace and non-effeminate war,
to separate: into a possibly violent night,
within a darker blue sight of twilight stars
moon glowing shadow from an off freeway urban eerie place.
They had explained themselves as frontline soldiers:
stockade smiles from ripped-off stripes on their faces,
while discussing death by bullet and their two-week army passes;
and my meditations on war and peace personal, I have nothing
better to do nature,
we split up like a below ground atomic explosion
and went our separate ways.

WRITTEN PRIOR TO 8 P.M. AT THE CAFE BABAR

He was sitting in the culinary near a big pot, empty, and a
coffee-drinking biker with a slight limp, playing a non-existent
accordion between his hands, and a big band leader's smile
between his swart hands and brown hair. He was trying to
release a smile after several years of plexiglas visits from a
pale pen pal called Rally who took estrogen like candy and
cried in a low yet hoarse voice near the prison visiting room
gum machine that wasn't working anymore. He was forcing his
celly to fast so he could stay heavy, above the cell of a man who
was trying to write his first and last pre-execution book: people
read about 'the man of death' in their local newspaper. 'Man of
death' was a quiet man, refusing to cry out to the guards for his
life. In other states they laughed at men about to die loudly,
and they laughed at men about to die quietly; they beat them
up wearing white gloves that made no noise while they bruised
flesh of death.

HIS DAD'S OLD CAR

His Dad's old car
now a desert has-been
stopped at an on-ramp
past six other hitchhikers;
he, driver lean, called out
"Get in" and I did
on a gray, I-have-lain-
on-this-ramp-three-days-
without-a-car-stopping
day,
and we roared off.
He made money poaching
the desert, buying a bag
of drugs, under the seat of
this broken-down car,
neither of us having money for
food. Ninety miles an hour through
unrelieved sand until the
battery ran down and he dropped
me off, hurrying me out of his
baby before looking for a
station.
Bet Dad was a conservative;
bet the seat sprung for roll
of bills, when the electric
window rolled down, and Father
said to a repairman, "Got a
coil coming out of this seat,"
and the repairman saying "We got
seats from that year, drive her
in."

The car drove off. He didn't cut
the engine. Left me there after one
hundred miles. Said he's be back
if he could buy another battery;
never saw him again. Another car
stopped in a few hours for me.

HITCHHIKING THROUGH

He was hitchhiking through
three or four states
with an orange in his coat
pocket and not much else.
Owned a store in the Deep
South, he told me, thumbing
back to it. We ate berries
by the side of the road
off bushes, he grinned at me
and said, "Nice breakfast."
Got caught in strong winds
with him, tried putting up
a small green plastic tent.
No trees for its hunched
spine rope to tie
around. He crawled out at
four in the morning. I saw
him three days later along
another road: "I got too cold
and left to stay warm." Never
saw him again after that.

WISDOM'S WELL

Once, in a wilderness of short, wind-wavering grass,
a barren space was brown as near evening's color;
I thought of symbols for chill night air:
hard soil broke up with a footstep creating dust;
I will fill in with a day's light, these motes of reality.

This is not wisdom's well,
with a shrug of spring days' sprig of wildflower stem,
covered in a fine coat of red embankment dust
floating on a surly wind circling itself like a freeway dustdevil,

or a hot sun upon the throat of a hitchhiker staring up thirsty,
who has stumbled on the truth of nature like a stubbed toe,
and this pain was so vast inside him, he knew it meant
nothing.

I am going to leave as winter's first leaf,

on an updraft of fog I will clear my sight
until the sun of day is warm to my root.

There I will grow upon my nature;
until this is a language stalked by years,
and not a crawling instant.

Night dropped everything and ran:
I could not run faster than horror,
hard packed dirt strewn with granite gray rock
and branch-thick twigs under my sleeping body.

Once, laying on cardboard, I closed my eyes
pretending to sleep, and a tramp man
walking a cement opening near me
wanted a soft hat that had been given
me easy. He grabbed a rock
after stepping into this opening
and held it over my head,
thinking about smashing mine in the cold
night of his heart beating enough
for both of us, the warm night's blood
vision from his cold eyes, freezing us
both into statues of human loneliness,
joined together in a form of life
and death's kind thought for each
other. I did not move. He had a
kind thought, and let me live.

I sleep there no more:

was night afraid of death in me?
Morning's light holds a sun
down in the earth arising
out of the root of my
thought, from this ground
that has held me living;

a psychic wound red as sunset
or sunrise.

Night was clear spoken wind
night had no breath except itself
night gave in to a blue sky
night slept inside space.

I awoke and this darkness
of night had spaced itself
elsewhere.

A STEP AWAY

A step away from the poverty ladder
up to the roof of the poverty world
screaming up to the stars at night
until there is a film over my eyes,
and I cannot see the world in all its
miserable actuality.

The ladder has fallen over
because I live indoors now
and cannot climb the poverty ladder anymore.
In truth I agree with those who say that,
they are not speaking from their true view of the world:
for they know I have climbed the poverty ladder
too many times for this ladder to be removed, or not removed,
at the whim of the world's indolence, or work.

NOW HEAR
THIS

LISA RADON

NOW HEAR THIS
Lisa Radon
(1992)

CLAUSTROPHOBE

as the elevator ascends
the floor rises faster than the ceiling
and the space i stand in grows shorter and shorter
and the walls shrink inward
the walls are closing in

i'm a secretary
we have an excellent health plan
you'll come in to work a half an hour early, won't you lisa?
in that split second
i look down to see
the jaws of the steel trap close in slow motion
on my leg

narrow metro train
packed with people
the only air is air that someone else has already
breathed or sweated or perfumed
but i breathe anyway, faster and faster
trying to find the one breath of unadulterated air
as the train plunges underground
into a tunnel barely bigger than the train
outside the windows, the walls of the tunnel are inches from
the train
i try not to look
'cause i know if i do
i'll see that
the walls are closing in

every time i have to say, "i can't, i have to work"
every time the bills arrive
every morning on my way to work at 7:30 on BART
     after a late drinking night
every birthday

the skyscrapers grow around me
getting closer, arching inward
in the middle of the street
i am sandwiched between two cold concrete masses
the walls
the walls

i try to escape
i run through a door to a hallway

but it is not a hallway
it is a closet
and the minute i enter
the door slams behind me
and the clothes, practical clothes, start moving toward me
from all directions
closer
closer till my face is buried in navy blue suits
and i am being smothered by professional blouses
strangled by conservative gold chains and strings of pearls

jill's getting married
debbie's pregnant
bill bought a house
"but they're so young!" i scream
"they're your age dear," my mom says
and i'm sweating now
and i'm backed up against the wall
and the other wall is inches from my face

the faces are all around me now
the wall of flames closes in
there is no escape
"happy birthday, sweetie"
"i had two children by the time i was your age"
"you're looking more like your mother every day"
"you should start planning for retirement now dear,
you're never too young"
"you've lived a quarter of your life"
"it's all downhill from here"
the flames suck away all the air
i can't breath
i stomp on the flames

i remember only yesterday
i slept through class and went to the beach in the middle of
    the week
my weekends started on thursday
i had all the time in the world
i came home early from school to watch star trek
i was batman on his bat-cycle
        screaming down the hill on my three-speed
i could do a double flip off the low board
i climbed the biggest tree in the valley
i remember dick and jane like it was on the page before
hemingway

looking forward to the day when i could eat whatever i wanted
go to bed whenever i wanted
thinking the middle schoolers were so big and scary
i had the best crayon set of all my friends

i just need a little time
i just need
five minutes to catch my breath

THE GIRL WITH THE EIGHT-TRACK BRAIN

i got an eight-track inside my brain
they don't make eight tracks any more
but i got one
up here
only it's broken
and that's the problem, see
because it'll just switch from track to track
every now and then
and i can't do anything about it
and it makes it really hard to concentrate
or have a conversation
or just finish anything really
'cause i'm doing one thing then i think about something else
and forget
the first thing
so like i'm always going around with my sweater half buttoned
because i skipped tracks in the middle of getting dressed
and i'm reading two books and watching the tube
and having one conversation with a friend and another one
with myself
burning toast
and hearing music in my head
and thinking about what's *under* all those manhole covers

and never mind trying to write
i just get confused

i've got a broken eight track inside my head
and
i don't know
if this involuntary channel switching
is like some t.v. generation mutation

like remote control run amok
or if it's just me

and it's not just the same eight tracks all the time
which would simplify things
i mean if it was just like:
sex, beer, food, scotch tape, aardvarks,
trailer parks, the meaning of life, and giant squid
i could probably get used to that
but there are always new tracks

and i don't know where they come from
maybe there's this deck of topic cards
and some little guy in there picks one out
and the next thing you know
i'm making love and   derail
i'm thinking about
drano

and this is fine and very entertaining when i am by myself
i can go on for hours and never be bored
but it makes social interaction very difficult

it's embarrassing
i'll be talking to someone about something really serious
you know,
like some heavy family scene
and i think *waffles*
how i haven't had waffles in ages
and they're talking and talking
and if i don't watch it
i'll say something like,
 "hey, do you like waffles?"
so i have to be careful

ya, my train of thought runs on eight tracks
i can't help it
i've got a broken piece of 70's junk hardware in my head
and it probably has a led zep sticker on it
'cause that would just figure

LOST AND FOUND

i was at the lost and found the other day
because, well, it seems i had lost my head
and i knew that someone would turn it in
because what would anyone want with my head if they did find it
or whoever found it would be scared shitless
 and want to get rid of it as soon as possible

so anyway, like i say, i was at the lost and found the other day
you wouldn't believe what they got there
i mean, i think most people don't even know it's there
this big warehouse full of lost and found
ya, you wouldn't believe what they got in there

first thing i see is this old man in a folding chair
rocking and mumbling to himself
and when i walk past him
i hear him spewing numbers
the old lady behind the counter said
he had calculated pi in his head to the 83rd digit
so far
and was constantly repeating it over and over
until he took some time to calculate it to the next digit
then he'd start in on reeling off the whole thing again
seems he'd lost his head a long time ago
but when he came in to the lost and found to get it
they didn't have it
he said he'd just wait then
and he'd been sitting there
by the front desk of the lost and found for twelve years
calculating pi to the 83rd digit

this was the lost and found
there were huge dark piles all around the perimeter of the
warehouse
blue and brown and black left socks
there was a huge bin full of ball point pens
another full of scraps of paper, napkins,
matchbooks with phone numbers written on them
and one more filled to overflowing with a million key rings full
  of keys
and sixteen year old virginities all over the place
and 45 year old mid-life crisis sufferers
running around pulling on their hair
going "what's it all about?"

or just moping on corners
and alienated suburban teenagers writing in their woe-is-me
  diaries
and runaways giving themselves jailhouse tattoos
there were a few nature boys decked in hiking gear
who had been plucked from the sierra's just as they were
beginning to
contemplate the moral implications of cannibalism

the lost and found
and i'm not positive but i swear i saw amelia earhardt, jim
morrison and elvis
talking at a little table in one corner

LOST!
there dogs and cats running around yapping and mewing
named muffin and poochy
cute ones like the ones they have on those
handwritten
help find me
he was my best friend
lost dog and kitty posters
you see on telephone poles

and FOUND!
there was a guy sweeping the floors
sweating and drooling in some sort of fit
and hollering about jeeezus and sinners
apparently he'd found god
but the lost and found staff had determined that he'd
subsequently lost his
head and so convinced him to stick around until it turned up

out in back there were countless cars with out of state license
plates and
plenty of rentals
and one bus from idaho all full of tourists
who had become lost in the city
looking for lombard street and fisherman's wharf

anyway, my head didn't turn up there at the lost and found
turns out i didn't actually lose it
when i screamed at the client
IF YOU WOULD JUST KEEP YOUR SHORTS ON FOR ONE
FUCKING

MINUTE MR. FITZWINKLE, I WOULD BE MORE THAN
HAPPY TO
ASSIST YOU
OR
YOU CAN SIMPLY GO FUCK YOURSELF
and ripped the phone out of the wall
then found another phone
and called up everyone who'd ever pissed me off and told 'em
exactly what i thought

nah, i didn't lose my head
it couldn't near be called lost
compared to what i found
in the lost and found
nah
i didn't lose my head
just misplaced it

REALITY WORLD

reality world
i found it
or i thought i found it
reality world
it was there on California Street near Larkin
and there was this big sign
reality world
and i thought *great*
finally
and i was so excited
because, you know, now they're all excited about this virtual
reality that is
like reality except in a computer, you know, like pretend reality
except
you put on this helmet and earphones and stuff and it's
supposed to be
like you're in this pretend world inside the computer
virtual reality
shit, like this is something new
man, we're surrounded by virtual reality
i mean, what is tv if it isn't virtual reality
i mean, it looks like real people,
or what we are supposed to

believe are real people
livin' out their virtual realities
in their little virtual homes
on their virtual little streets
or those real life adventure, true crime shows
where its like its a real crime story or whatever except they
"reenact" it for
television
and books are virtual reality...
even if they're non-fiction and talk about reality, you know,
that isn't
reality
it's just a reporting of it
even the news is virtual reality...
almost the whole real story of what pretty much really
happened
and grape flavoring
which is artificial, but it's so real that
you taste this grape lollipop or grape drink
and someone says, "what does it taste like?"
and you say, "grape"
but it has nothing to do with the real taste of grapes
so it's like virtual grape
it's so hard to tell what's real from what isn't
the blurry lines
truth and sham
and near reality
and so that's why i was so excited when i found it
you know, reality world
without any deep, time-consuming philosophical discourse
i flipped
and i thought
it's in there
it's all in there
maybe plato's forms are even in there and not just theoretical
reality world was closed
but i was gonna go up and hunker down in that doorway
and wait for it to open in the morning
i didn't care
8, 9 hours
what's too long to wait to get into reality world, huh?
i was wondering why they were advertising with this big sign
cause if everybody knew about reality world
even if they were scared of what they'd find
they'd wanna at least check it out a little
you know, just to see

but then i see
Mrs. Peter's ESP, Psychic, Palmistry and Tarot Card Readings
10 a.m. to 10 p.m. with a big red sign, right next door
and so i figure reality world's sign is to, you know, distinguish
and make sure nobody thinks they're like associated
but as i get closer to reality world
i see pictures of houses
like the ones on t.v.
in the windows
and i'm starting to wonder
'cause it's looking pretty virtual
and i'm scared
and i get up there
and, man, what a dope
it's fuckin'
realty world
and you know i knew it wasn't gonna be that easy

DEAR BARBIE,

I want to thank you for all that I leaned from you.
Lessons about American values, like the value of perfect skin,
white teeth, blond hair. You were the role model for me and
millions of girls like me.

You showed us that we could have it all: Barbie Townhouse,
Barbie Sun & Fun Pool, Barbie Speed Buggy, closet full of
designer fashions, and, of course, Ken, Mr. Right, who always
dressed nice, never farted or cussed, never stood you up, and
always did exactly what we girls told him to do.

If only, we thought, we could grow up to be just like you:
the ideal woman

36-24-36, with breasts so perfect, high, and pointy,
you never had to wear a bra
permanent lipstick, clear blue eyes, natural blond hair
legs and armpits that never needed shaving
and a head filled with air (I know because I looked when I
accidentally popped your head off while dressing you in yet
another beautiful outfit).

You were always dressed for the occasion.

You never got split ends or dandruff or cellulite or zits.
And after years and years, you had no wrinkles, and no sagging
anywhere.

Thank you, Barbie, on behalf of all my sisters, for years of
futile dieting, women's mag beauty tips, self-help books,
encounter groups, Richard Simmons/Jane Fonda, and $100 an
hour therapy... all inspired by your shining example.

Just once, just once, I'd like to see you sweat. I'd like to see you
wearing a polyester uniform behind the counter at Burger
Kind. I'd like to see your makeup smeared and your hair
messed up. I'd like to see you walk in on Ken and Skipper.
I'd like your car to break down and then I want you to lose your
Burger King job and have to move out of the townhouse!!!!

I'd like to rip off your perfectly shaped legs and shove your feet
in the neck-hole in your rubber head.

I'm glad now, that my little brother, Ben, blew you up with an
M-80 when I was 9 (although I was traumatized at the time
and took my revenge on that fuzzhead GI Joe). In fact,
I wish I would have lit the match myself.

Sincerely,

Feeling much better now

WEIRDOS AND FREAKS

you've seen them
they've probably even thought about talking to you, too
but they don't
they talk to me
they're nuts and they seek me out
and sometimes i want to pop them but usually i love them
always total strangers
total freaks
or just tilted
i love them
i collect them

has anyone ever opened a conversation with you
by silently sliding a bazooka joe comic across the bar?

16th and mission
loopy central
short lady with few brown broken teeth and squinty eyes and
big scabs
on her face comes up and asks what the cafeteria over there
serves
i'm sorry i don't know
she asks for a quarter for food
okay
god bless you
what is your name
i tell her
ooo, my youngest sister's named lisa marie
she peers up close into my face
whuss yer middle name
god! i tell here elena but she gets it wrong
she smiles her no-tooth smile up at me, "lisa nina thass pretty
my names laurie ann, pleased to meet you"
she sticks out probably the dirtiest hand i have ever seen
i shake it, fine.
well, take care, i say
keep smiling, she says
i smile

i'm waiting to get off the train
an old black man looks up at me
"go forth and do great things"
and wow, i feel touched by god

and the guy selling pot out of his dirty sneaker

and
"hey, you got a cigarette?
ya, i'm trying to quit...
well, i did quit
they don't let you smoke 'em in jail"
"here"
"uh thanks," he says then quick steps to catch up with me
i keep walking and try to look like i'm engrossed in reading
what's printed
on the inside of the matchbook... "How to Get Published"
"hey, whatcha readin'?" i hand it to him
now can i go?

"hey, did you know that spiders have their penis in their leg?"
he wiggles
his arm. "ya, i read it in omni"
"omni's cool," i say, "but i don't buy it"
"ya, i don't buy it either,
but you can read it down at the seven eleven
ya, in their legs.
hey, where do you work?"
i wave my arm in some general direction and say, "over there"
"oh what do you do?"
"i type."
"really, i knew a girl once who typed
her fingers flew so fast" he demonstrates
"wish i could type
i bet you make a lot of money
i get $300 a month from the government,
ya, 'cause i can't get a job
'cause i'm, you know, manic depressive
oh, you gotta go?
okay, well hey thanks for the cigarette
ya see you around"
now there's a way to impress women. tell them you've been in
   jail and
you can't get a job 'cause you're manic depressive all within the
   first
three minutes of conversation. i think about going back and
recommending he read Carnegie's *How to Win Friends and
Influence People*.

i'm waiting for a bus at two thirty-three in the morning.
i sit down next to him.

"whattimedyagot
whattimedyagot
yaineverwearawatch
buscomesattwofortyfive
alwaystwofortyfive

"yathebuscomesattwofortyfive
whattimedyasayitwas
yatwofortyfive
ineverwearawatch
bus'llcomealongnowanytime
comesattwofortyfive"

i'm taking a cab.

170

i'm at a bus stop
there's a guy standing in a phone booth
"yes, it's all coming clear...it's all clear to me now."
"you know," he says to me...
"you and me, we could make beautiful music together,
but you know what?
we won't
and you wanna know why?
because satan loves you more than you love me."

they tell me things
strange things

"do you think that it is a more terrible thing
that you are smoking those even though they are the number one
preventable cause of death in the United States
or that i am sitting here drinking this when my father's an
   alcoholic?"
jeez. "buy you an orange juice?" i say
"no thanks. i'm filing for bankruptcy, you know..."

...and on and on...

i am a magnet for the weird
i look in the mirror very carefully to see if somewhere on my
face there is
a big sign reading, "tell me everything."
i sometimes think that they see some soft spot in me that they
   can dig
into to leave their story
but maybe it's just that they sense that, to a point, i appreciate
   madness a
little more than the next guy
sometimes i guess they're trying to connect or just say, "hey
   look at me."
and mostly i think it's cool because i don't have a t.v. and this is
   better than
anything they got on there anyway

APATHY TO GO

this is the voice of my generation
it's coming from a
guy wearing a nixon mask, a silver lamé shirt
and no pants
he's screaming louder than a jet engine
and you can't hear a word he's saying
over the guitars

this is the voice of the absurd
the pro-castro forces on one side of 18th
and the anti-castro expatriates on the other
yelling and chanting and brandishing
hand-scrawled signs at one another
and they may as well have been yelling
tastes great
less filling
for the relevance and effect it all had

i'm tired of walking around with rocks in my pockets
global socio-politico-eco-depresso rocks
regional conflict front-page economic plague mondo rocks
the size of gibraltar
pulling my shoulders down
a 25-year-old hunchback
walking on her knees

so when that little voice in my head says
hey, baby, who cares
everything's gonna go on
no matter what you do
now take that jacket off, girl
you got rocks in your pockets
let me buy you a beer
i say okay
and buy myself a beer

who's got the remote control
let's change the channel

i'm hanging a do not disturb sign
around my neck
i'm not a communist, not a socialist or a capitalist
i'm not an anarchist
i'm an apathist

my philosophy can be summed up in one word
"so?"

this is the voice of the times
it's saying
hey sister can you spare some change
and i can
and i do
the marrying man, the have a nice evening lady, the happy guy,
it's easier to care about a person than an issue

mail all your propaganda about your causes
in a big box to me
put a tag on it
do not open 'til the year 2002
maybe then i'll feel like doing something about it
hell, maybe then i'll feel like talking about it
likely it will have been resolved or forgotten by then
without my help

it's not that i don't care
well
ya, it is, sort of

i'm just going to hang myself on a coat hook here
and i'll come down when you
figure it all out

i'm an isolationist party of one
yes, and i'd like a window table
if it's not too much trouble
where i can keep an eye on what's going on
although my food may be more interesting

i do get mad as hell sometimes
but in the end i don't really care enough
to do anything about anything

everybody keeps getting whipped into a froth
by the media blender
over one issue or another
that everyone will completely forget in a month
but they're still stuck with those whale and dolphin and
free tibet bumper stickers
i'm convinced that everything that's gonna happen will happen
regardless of whether i take a stand

or sit down
or cast a ballot
or throw a bomb
or whine

i'm leading the charge of the revolution of apathy
ready now
okay
sit down and order another beer
let's play yahtzee
you go first

ZUCCHINI

and other stories

Jon Longhi

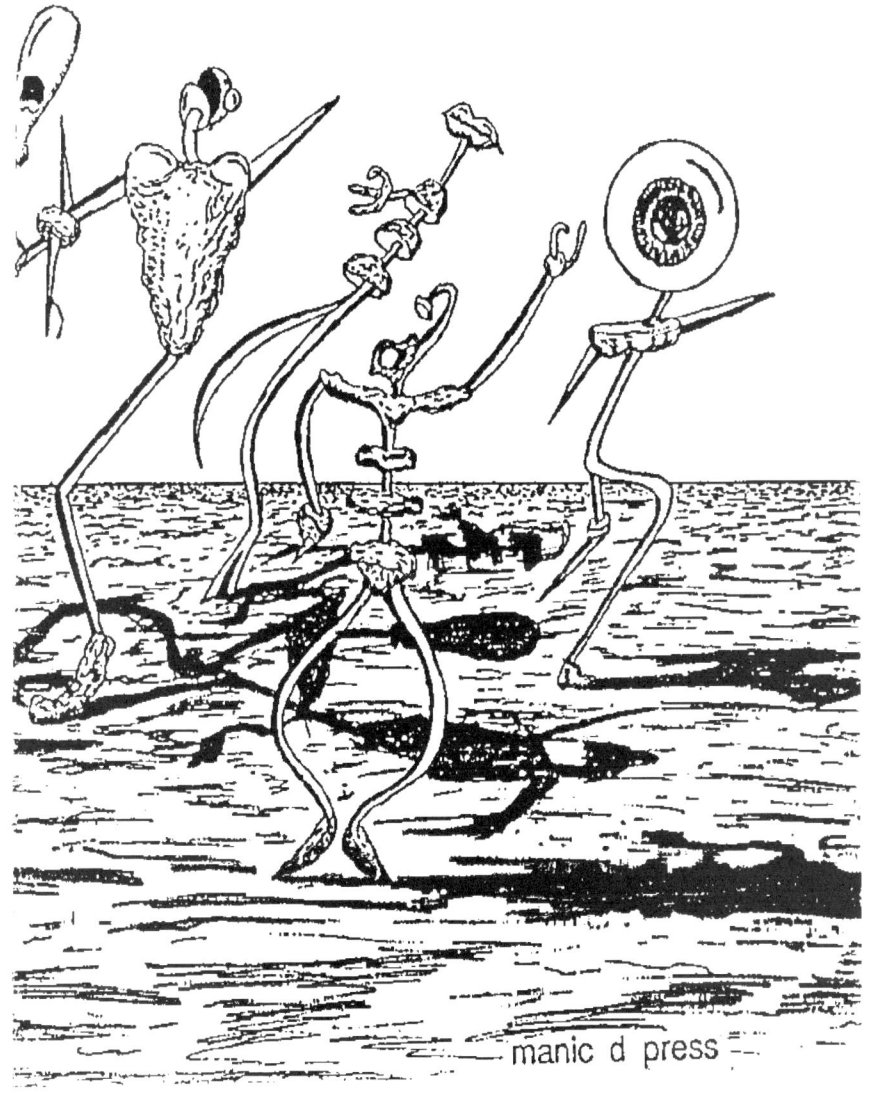

manic d press

ZUCCHINI AND OTHER STORIES
Jon Longhi
(1990)

BIGFOOT

I had this friend who worked as a clown in the Ringling Brothers Circus but he had to quit because he hurt his foot doing a double flip over two elephants. After that he walked with a limp. So he was an out-of-work clown who walked with a cane and even though his painted face had been crying, now he really hit the skids and did the weed and acid till he blew it.

Got it into his head he wanted to see Bigfoot and spent six months camped out in the Rockies. When he finally saw the modern missing link, it scared him till he started screaming and ran off down the mountain, tripped and hurt his bum foot but got up and ran another half mile before he injured his other foot. When the paramedics brought him down to the hospital, both of them had swelled up so big, they broke open his shoes like seed pods.

Even though he got better and could almost walk fine, the swelling never went down. So he had to buy huge shoes. Now when he walks around, people think he's working as a clown all the time.

PASCAL

I once knew a guy named Pascal who was a dumb anarchist skatepunk. He would latch onto any lefty idea that came along and ride it down the toilet bowl. Last year he became a militant vegetarian. It was a really political thing for him and he would walk into restaurants and start screaming at people for eating steak. Then he vandalized a Burger King and spray painted "Vegetarianism Now" all over its front windows. He claimed it was to protest the fact that they served hamburgers but nobody had the heart to tell him it was all just soybean now. Nothing like a radical vegetarian terrorist. They're worse than the PLO.

Then he made his most desperate move. He bought an AK-47 and two handguns and took a grocery store hostage. The shoppers ran out in terror as he barricaded himself in the produce section behind a wall of carrots and oat sacks stacked like sandbags. When the police surrounded the place, he went up to the front window to make a statement. He held a gun up to a head of lettuce and threatened to shoot. Then he liberated the hotdogs and sausage links from the freezer section and demanded that they be mailed to India. After he died in a hail of gunfire, he became a martyr for cows the world over. Sometimes you still see his "Wanted" poster in post offices - a fugitive from the FDA.

Pascal became dead meat so red meat could live.

TWO-HEADED HEIFERS

I remember a few years ago I was at the Harrington State Fair. It was redneck rodeo heaven, with parking lots full of pickup trucks and a smell of watermelons hanging over everything. Produce contests, six legged pigs and two headed heifers. Bull wrestling, cowboy hats, and lots of Big Red chewing tobacco.

I was standing in the dusty parking lot, when these two dudes drove up in an El Camino. "Hey man, you want to see something special?" they said and waved me over to the car. In the backseat lay a girl around seventeen. She was passed out, and her jeans and panties were pulled down around her ankles. There was a ball of lint on her pubic hair. I gawked.

"Yeah," said one of the dudes. "She's all fucked up. Passed out about three hours ago, so we pulled down her drawers, and have been driving her all over the county showing her to people." He took another suck off his Budweiser and roared off across the parking lot toward a group of guys heading for the front gate.

I just stood there hoping no one would see my erection.

HIP BONES

God we humped for days, two mindless fuck monkeys going at it like we'd just discovered the real secret of evolution. Weeks went by, we didn't get out of bed, having pizza and drinks delivered in, our friends and jobs drifting away while we just kept screwing.

Swimming through the submarine depths of flesh, occasionally rising up to the flannel sheets on the surface for a gasp of air and a glance at the window to see if it was night or day. And then we'd go down again. Into that perfect rhythm. Eventually there wasn't enough time to eat, and we wasted away while the world fell down around us, but we didn't care cause there was only that thing.

Once we'd eroded away our genitals, muscles and skin, there were just two sexual skeletons banging their bones in a wild percussive jam, till femurs and hand joints rattled cross the floor.

Two years later, when our friends came to look for us, all they found was the broken bed. In its center, two battered hip bones still lightly tapping against each other.

SOME ORGASM

I remember a girl I knew who once had a two-hour orgasm. It was back before AIDS, in the time of orgies, and we were having a foursome, two of each sex in a wild frenzied grope and slide in her dark dorm room. After we had all collapsed into sweat and were laying quiet, softly stroking each other, she still made little wheezing sounds. We all got up and took a group piss and shower, in the stall with barely enough room to hold us. Then we dressed and went out to a party.

The other three of us tried to get picked up but she kept walking around with a worried look on her face, and locked herself in the bathroom for long periods of time making little feline noises. Finally she pulled me aside and said, "Jon, I don't know if I'm going crazy, but I can't hold it together, uh uhh, whatever happened with us back in my room is still going on for me," and she began to moan.

I reached my hand into her pants and felt her mound. The clitoris was swollen to the size of a baby's penis, juice flowed freely down her legs and I realized she kept having to come back to the bathroom to wipe. She asked me to walk her back to her room because she couldn't be like this in a social situation.

I, of course, said yes, anticipating more hot sex, but when we got back to the privacy of her room, she didn't even need me. Just sat on her bed alone and screamed for forty-five minutes in long shuddering waves, while I sat in a chair and watched her. God, was I jealous. When it was finally over, she collapsed exhausted on the bed and promptly fell asleep. So I went back to the party to see if I could get some more.

A CURRENT AFFAIR

It is not sure exactly when Howard Fergusson became addicted to electricity. It might have been in the fifties when he first received electroshock therapy. He had been depressed for months and his psychiatrist suggested that it might improve his attitude. When they affixed the metal ring to his skull like a crown of thorns and applied the conductive gel, Howard felt transcendent, enervated, and special, a new initiate into some dark desire. Then the doctors threw the switch and everything became a white glare, his entire musculature tensed upward in an arc and he came before his penis could even get erect. Suddenly Howard Fergusson's life had new meaning. All the cobwebs in his brain had been swept away in one bolt of lightning. The doctors noticed that his mood had improved immediately. He was downright jovial. As he left the hospital, he was laughing and shaking hands.

When he got back to the silence and privacy of his apartment Howard got down to work. He glued two squares of aluminum foil to his chest. With scissors he cut an extension cord in half and taped the flayed wires to the squares of aluminum foil. Then he stuck the plug into a wall socket. The jolt threw him back against the living room wall where he passed out for a few moments. When Howard came to, all his chest hair had been burned off and there was sperm on his face.

He kept doing it. Three or four times a week he would plug himself into a wall socket. It gave him a special excitement when the jolt was accompanied by a tiny whiff of burnt flesh. As the years went by, his torso became covered with small welts and electrical scars and he eventually ceased altogether his searches for female companionship. He found wall outlets much more attractive and often had to suppress an erection when he saw someone changing a light bulb. His apartment grew cluttered with old appliances, torn circuit boards, transistors, and discarded TV sets. He had extra outlets installed. The utility bills grew with his electrical sexual hunger. Whenever he put in a new bulb he could not resist sticking his fingers into the empty socket.

After a two-year trade school, he became an electrician and began mixing business with pleasure. His skill was legendary and he received a lot of big contracts. Howard loved the work, and besides, it supplied him with large amounts of electronic equipment. The apartment began to look like the inside of a transistor radio as Howard combined all his many appliances, circuit grids, and cathode tubes into one huge apparatus. When friends asked him what it was, he called it a perpetual motion machine. You see Howard had found out that electricity was the only hope for the survival of the soul. It was transcendence. More than a regenerative force, it was the central spark of life itself. Howard began connecting his giant machine to lightning rods on the roof. Then one stormy night as the rods crackled and ball lightning drifted through his windows, Howard fired the electrodes and crawled into his machine, using his body as the final circuit in its web of current. All the furies of heaven and the power companies flowed into that apartment which glowed bright white and then dimmed in a pall of burnt flesh. Then all the other lights in New York City went out.

FISH TALE

It rained fish that day. The smoggy sky turned dark and scaly. Inside the thunderheads you could see the schools writhing about like embryos in a translucent egg. When the clouds hit New York City the skyscrapers gouged open their bellies and all those sea creatures spilled out on the window cleaners. Wall Street became a fish market as economy-minded executives began stuffing tunas into the trunks of their Audis. Sharks landed in the lake in Central Park, octopuses clung to the Statue of Liberty. Soon the gutters were clogged with dead fish and low-lying areas flooded as if the sea were reclaiming her prehistoric territory. Psychics claimed it was the harbinger of a new baby boom; most people thought it was the end of the world. Cats gorged themselves; winos ate fresh lobsters they had found in trash cans. Fish stew was the special of the day in all the restaurants on Broadway. Two planes were knocked from the sky: one by sea turtles, another by a school of trout. Since the fish storm happened on Friday, most Catholics took it as a sign from God that it was time to change their diets. But the Pope claimed that only the Devil tempts man with gifts of fish. At the stock market, fish prices tumbled, tartar sauce and lemon shares soared. Times Square whores hiked up their skirts as halibuts flopped about their red pumps. Someone called the New York Times and claimed this was scientific proof that Aqua Man and Marine Boy actually existed. Mayor Koch declared it a city holiday, Fish Day. New York truly was the city where anything could happen.

By evening, when the spring sun had burned the storm clouds to a haze, there rose from the scaly streets a stench that made a garbage strike seem like a perfume convention. Dead eyes stared at you from every gutter. Cats went rabid. Suddenly the Big Apple smelled rotten. The next morning New Yorkers hit rush hour wearing surgical masks. Everyone was a surgeon. The sewers became spawning grounds and whenever you turned on your tap minnows spewed from the faucet. Sea urchins trundled about the Village. Something fishy was going on. Had Moses moved to Soho? TV evangelists claimed it was God's way of punishing man for not donating more to them. By the next afternoon, the stench was so bad that even the garbage men were throwing up on the sidewalks. What was going on? We'd heard of it raining cats and dogs - but fish?

Finally an answer came from (of all places) the National Weather Service. The day before the storm a waterspout had touched down in the North Atlantic spawning grounds. Hundreds of tons of fish and sea life were sucked up the funnel into the sky. For nearly twenty-four hours the fish swam through the air, held aloft by near-hurricane turbulence as the storm moved inland. By the time it reached New York it was just a cloudburst and the net of winds spilled open. To this day, you can still find fish bones on rooftops.

YOU SHOULD SEE HOW MANY PEOPLE THINK THEY'RE RELATED TO DEAD JONESES

Grandmother died yesterday. Or at least we thought she did. The headline read: "CEMETERY SLAYING IS PROBED". An Elizabeth "Betty" Franklin murdered in a graveyard near Chester, PA. The 73-year-old woman had lived alone off Marsh Road north of Wilmington. She had worked as a librarian for 20 years and was shot during an apparent robbery. The women bled to death among the tombstones. My grandmother's name is Betty Franklin. She lives off Marsh Road north of Wilmington. Since the death of my grandfather 3 years ago, she has lived alone. She is 73 years old and had worked as a librarian for 20 years.

Why hadn't the police contacted us? Why did we have to find out about it from the papers? Me and my relatives called grandmother's house all afternoon but there was no answer. When we called the Police they told us that yes, a Betty Franklin had been murdered in Chester and they were trying to contact her next of kin. We told them that we were her relatives and asked for a list of the people who had called in so we would know which members of the family still had to be informed. There was a problem with the list. Some of the people on it weren't related to us. The police sergeant brushed it off. Problems like this often arise in the couple of days of confusion immediately following death. Especially with a name as common as Franklin. You should see how many people think they're related to dead Joneses, he said.

There were other similarities. After a short chase, police had arrested a 16-year-old boy who was driving Betty Franklin's car. There was no car at the scene of the murder. Her purse was missing. It was not until after they recovered the car that police could even tentatively identify the body. The stolen purse was in the back seat and the license in it apparently matched the dead woman's face. But they couldn't be sure. My grandmother has a 16-year-old boy from her neighborhood who does all her yardwork and often drives her car when her arthritis acts up. About twice a month she visits a graveyard near Chester because she has friends buried there.

But there were differences too. The obituary listed the wrong address. A typo? It also claimed she had never married. Grandma was married to Grandpa for 52 years. We clung to the hope that she was still alive, but most of the evidence pointed against it. According to the police it was still too early in the investigation for them to be sure of anything. Neither the front page article nor the obituary had printed a picture of the woman and the body had not been conclusively identified yet. I think her face had been messed up. My mother was driving up from Washington to determine whether or not the deceased was her mother. We had continued calling through the late afternoon but still had gotten no answer at Grandma's house. Things looked grim.

If Grandma was still alive it meant that for years she had been living oblivious of the fact that her doppelganger resided in the same neighborhood. A woman who shared her name, profession and habits. Neighbors must have mistaken the two of them. Maybe they thought the two Betty Franklins were one person who was extremely active and ever present. Friends must have been baffled when they showed up at the wrong Franklin residence by mistake. Letters ended up in the wrong boxes. But this was unlikely. Grandma's neighborhood was composed of catty old ladies for whom the substantive aspects of life had been replaced with idle chatter. Gossip drifted around those quiet streets like an omnipresent radar. The second Franklin could not have escaped its detection.

Around five o'clock I got a call from the police station. The woman who had been killed in the graveyard was most definitely not my grandmother. My mother had arrived at the coroner's office and did not recognize the corpse. As far as they know, my grandmother was still alive.

Finally I got through. It was dark. I could feel the hesitation in the hand that picked up the phone.

"Hello, Betty Franklin speaking."

"Grandma?"

"Yes, who's this?"

"It's David, your grandson David."

"David! Am I ever glad to hear your voice. I have had the strangest day. Everybody I met today told me I'm dead. When I got home from my flower arranging class people started showing up at the front door with funeral wreaths. Then when I talked to my neighbor Mrs. Trowel, she told me they arrested Smitty Fenhorn, the boy who does my yardwork, for murdering me. Oh I've had the most horrible day. Was up all night with nightmares. Kept dreaming I was lost in a graveyard and I couldn't find my way out. And then this morning I can't find my purse anywhere. Someone must have stolen it."

"Now just calm down, Grandma," I said. "Everything's OK now. Just calm down, remember your heart. You were on the front page of the paper today, put us in quite a whirl, quite a whirl."

"Oh really, that's wonderful will you read me the article? Things have been so hectic today, I haven't gotten a chance to pick up a paper. "

I read down the column of newsprint. Things fell into place. Grandma's breathing became rapid and hoarse.

"Calm down Grandma," I said. "It's not you."

"What do you mean, it isn't me," she shrieked. "Who else could it be? It's me! It's Me!"

I tried to calm her down but it was useless. She was beyond reason. I heard her tug an icy moan into her chest. Something big and soft hit the floor. Then there was just the tap tap tap of the loose receiver knocking against a table leg.

We buried Grandma in the cemetery near Chester, among her friends. No one had expected it. It had happened so suddenly. The mourners dressed in black made a tight ring around the grave. At the same time, on the other end of the cemetery, an identical circle was clustered around the grave of Betty Franklin.

IMMIGRANTS

For years my grandfather was just a check that arrived each Christmas in the mail. No personal note or card, just a simple signing away of money. My father mumbled of personal differences but these were never articulated into a palpable hatred that could have revolved our dinner table. That at least would have been something to remember him by. But they remained just mumblings, vague grunts of anger, and whenever we pressed my father for details he promptly dropped the whole subject. We did not see my grandfather once in the entire decade before his death. We missed his slow deterioration into cancer, his final days in a plastic tent. Though unaware, maybe we were already being pushed away by that adverse magnetism that all the afflicted radiate. He was a hard man. An Italian immigrant who would not surrender even though he died poor. His lack of education insured his lack of cash. My father was the one who went to college, got rich, and moved far away from his family.

Immigrants always want to leave something behind. Though my father moved upwards, not across seas, he still could not bear the reminder of my grandfather's seventh grade education. My father hid in country clubs and practiced his WASP. He was in India on business when grandfather died and he did not return for the funeral. Most of the family members made excuses not to go. Funerals are just too depressing for the modern world. We naturally move away from what is depressing, old, and afflicted until we have moved so far away that we have nothing to hang on to and sink to our own depths. I don't think he pushed us as much as we left. The living move on. He stayed put in a rest home for five years using the strength of his dying body to grow a flower bed. A square of blossoms like that on his grave.

In the end I was the only member of our family to attend his funeral. I am also poor and could not afford a suit of clothes. So I wore one of grandfather's old suits that his stricken body had grown too small to fit.

ZUCCHINI

zucchini

For years I couldn't stand to eat zucchini. It was because when I was growing up we always had a garden and for some reason the only thing that grew well for us was zucchini. We'd rake in bushels and bushels of it every year.

Each meal had 2 or 3 zucchini dishes. Fried zucchini with zucchini salad served with turkey stuffed with zucchini. Every day we'd be sent to school with zucchini sandwiches, thermoses full of hot zucchini soup, and a carton of zucchini milk.

We rode on a bus that ran on gasohol refined from zucchini. At the school (which was carved out of a huge zucchini with cellulose windows) we were taught history by a zucchini in a town where all the buildings were made of zucchini.

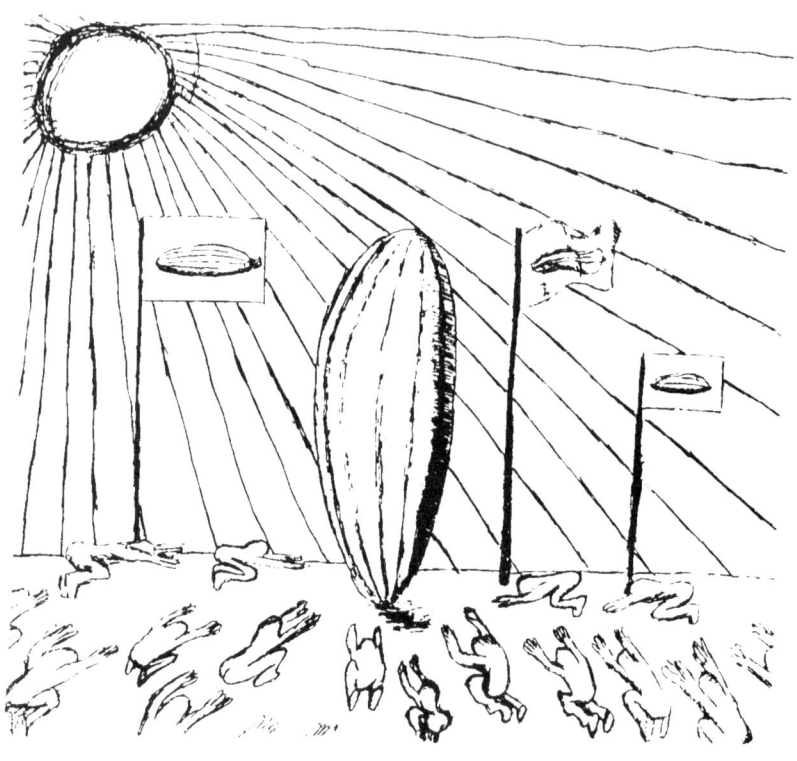

Even the candy was made of zucchini and the only thing you could buy in the stores was zucchini. The churches worshipped the phallic god Zucchini, and the government said that all you could think about was zucchini, and it became apparent that the land of the free had become the land of zucchini, and everywhere you looked it was zucchini, Zucchini, ZUCCHINI !

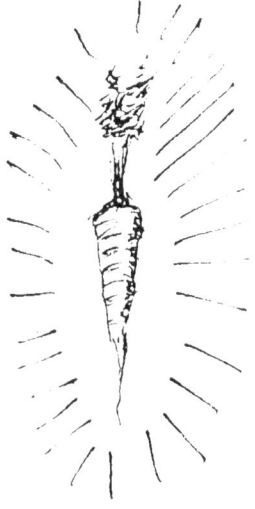

Till the next year. When all we could grow was carrots.

CORAZÓN DEL BARRIO

Poems by

Jorge Argueta

Corazón del Barrio

Manic D Press

CORAZON DEL BARRIO
Jorge Argueta
(1994)

ODA AL CAFÉ LA BOHEME

de todas partes del mundo
llegan a la Boheme
Una a una uno a uno
vienen llegando
La Boheme es las naciones unidas
ahí se habla español
francés italiano arabe
alemán inglés
y también mucha mierda
La Boheme es la casa
el refugio
el amparo de todos los exilados
el consuelo de los solos
y los locos

La Boheme ha sido el amor
para muchos
ahí se enamoró Ziggy de Greta
Rogelio de Patricia
Julia de Manolo
En la Boheme
nos hemos conocido todos
nos hemos amado todos
Muchos ya no están
como Alfredito "milonga"
el ya no vendrá jamas
a La Boheme como
lo hacía tarde a tarde
ahora esta bajo el suelo
de la pampa contando
sus chistes y sus cuentos
a los gauchos
Eleonora regressó a Venezuela
Luiggi volvió a Italia
y no volvimos a saber
qué fue de ellos.

La Boheme tiene
diecisiete años
Las mesas ya no son
las mismas
ni las tazas ni las paredes
De los empleados
sólo la Glena va quedando

ella esta ahí día tras día
con el dulce trueno
de su sonrisa
Glena conoce a todos
los qué llegan al café
lo qué toman
y a que horas llegan
Glena quiere tanto a La Boheme
el otro día que hable
con ella
me dijo con tristeza
en su sonrisa
cómo extrañaba
aquella vieja bohemia
la que ella sabe no volverá

ODE TO CAFE LA BOHEME

From all parts of the world
they come to La Boheme
One by one they arrive.

La Boheme is the United Nations.
Here they speak Spanish
French Italian Arabic
German English,
and also much shit.
La Boheme is the home,
the refuge,
the sanctuary of all those exiled,
the consolation of the lonely
and the mad.

La Boheme has meant love
for many.
Ziggy and Greta fell in love here,
Rogelio and Patricia,
Julia and Monolo.
At La Boheme
all were known,
all were loved.
Many are no longer there,
Like Alfredito "milonga"
he will never visit La Boheme
like he did every afternoon.

Now he's under the soil
of Argentina's pampa
telling his jokes and his stories
to the gauchos.
Eleonora went home to Venezuela,
Luiggi returned to Italy
and we never heard from them
again.

La Boheme is seventeen years old.
The tables are not the same
nor are the cups or the walls.
Of all the waitresses
only Glena has stayed

She's there, day after day
with sweet thunder in her smile.
Glena knows all those
who come to the café
what they drink
what time they arrive
Glena has great love for La Boheme.
The other day
when I spoke with her
she told me
with sadness in her smile
of how she missed
the old bohemia
she knows will never return.

JAIME

El viejo Jaime era simplemente Jaime
Jamás en La Boheme se conoció su
apellido
pero todos le decían Jaime cubano
Jaime era cubano, bién cubano
hablaba de literatura barroca
y elogiaba a Carpentier
"Muchacho es que en la manera
en que ese hombre usa el lenguaje
eso es rumba chico vaya
que quiere que te diga"

Jaime al escuchar un son que le
gustaba,
se paraba inmediatamente
adoptaba posición como de boxeador
con sus brazos doblados frente al pecho
comenzaba a deslizarse sonriendo
entre las mesas y los que compraban
Jaime parecía alegre, muy alegre
Jaime, el Viejo Jaime
como todavía le dice José el argentino
llegaba a La Boheme por las mananas
tomaba café estilo cubano
Y fumaba cigarros Camel
Jaime había salido de Cuba
allá por los sesentas
y decía que no volvería
pero quería estar cerca de la isla

Un buen día sin decir adios a nadie,
pero ni a José el argentino,
su mejor amigo, Jaime se desapareció.
Algunos piensan que se fue a Miami,
otros que se murió.

JAIME

Old Jaime was simply Jaime
No one in La Boheme knew his last name
so everybody called him Jaime the Cuban.
Jaime loved being a Cuban.
He liked to talk about baroque literature
and of Alejo Carpentier he would expound
The way that man uses
language is like rumba,
what else can I say?"

Old Jaime started to dance
when he heard a song that reminded him of Cuba
Old Jaime would stand up immediately
adopt the stance of a boxer
with his arms bent in front of his chest
and smiling he would begin to dance
swinging himself
happily and freely

between the tables.
Jaime seemed happy, very happy.
Jaime, Old Jaime
as always chatted with José the Argentinean
he came to La Boheme in the mornings
ordering his espresso Cuban style
and smoking Camel cigarettes.
Jaime left Cuba in the sixties
and he used to say he would never go back,
yet would like to be close to the island.

One fine day without saying goodbye to anyone
not even to José the Argentinean
his best friend, Old Jaime disappeared.
Some guess he went to Miami,
to die near his island.

MIGUEL PEREZ

Miguel Perez
llegó desde la pampa
a La Boheme
Pequeño
moreno
cara fruncida
ojos dulces

Miguel Perez
se ríe todo el tiempo
fuma como un demonio
habla del Che
discute de política
se rié fumando

Miguel Perez
estuvo preso
del '76 al '79
en Argentina
"Che, vos sabés,
lo que es estar encerrado
tres años?"

Luego se ríe
Miguel fuma
se ríe
como si fuera
su manera de olvidar

Miguel es bondadoso
su barba es una flor
lo metieron preso
-Ay que dolor
sin ver el cielo
-Ay que dolor
sin escuchar el mar

Miguel Perez
siempre va a venir
a La Boheme
eso me alegra
A mi me encanta
su apellido
porque yo también
soy Perez

MIGUEL PEREZ

Miguel Perez
from the Argentinean pampa
arrived
at La Boheme
small
dark skinned
frowning face
sweet eyes

Miguel Perez
is always smiling
smokes like hell
speaks of Che
discusses politics
laughs with a smile

Miguel Perez
was held in jail
in Argentina
from '76 to '79

"Che," he says
in his accent,
"Do you have any idea
what it's like
to be kept in jail
for three years?"

Later when he tells the story
he smokes
and smiles
as if it was his way
of forgetting

Miguel is very kind,
his beard is a flower.
They put him in jail
-Oh, what pain
without hearing the ocean
-Oh, what pain
without seeing the sky
Miguel Perez
will always come
to La Boheme
It makes me happy
to know this
I love his name
because I'm Perez too

ALFONSO TEXIDOR

Alfonso Texidor
llega al café a las once
pero no bebe café
bébe vino rojo todo el dia

Usa gorras de marinero
corbata de muchos colores
con camisa azul

Alfonso Texidor
es negro delgado
ama la salsa

pero no puede bailarla
ama la poesía
y la declama
con todo el ritmo de su voz

Alfonso Texidor
negro puertorriqueño
corazón de niño
cuando tiene dinero
invita a todo al que llega a La Boheme

Alfonso Texidor
es muy sincero
y si alguien
lo jode mucho
en seguida
lo manda
a cortar cana.

ALFONSO TEXIDOR

Alfonso Texidor
comes by the café at eleven
but he doesn't drink coffee
he sips red wine all day

A sailor's cap
a multi-colored tie
his shirt a night-sky blue

Alfonso Texidor
thin and dark
loves salsa
but he cannot dance
He loves poetry
and he reads it
with the rhythm in his voice

Alfonso Texidor
Dark Puerto Rican
Heart of a child
When he has money
all are invited as he comes to La Boheme

Alfonso Texidor

frank, bitingly honest
Should anyone attempt
to jibe him
he will
immediately
send them off
to cut cane

ODA A BENJAMIN FERRERA

Por ser honesto y por haber hecho
chiste de la manera en qué consiguió su
"cheque de loco"

Para no trabajar
Benjamín Ferrera
se hizo pasar por loco
y engañó a todos
los psiquiatras
del Hospital General
de San Francisco
"Karpov me está
esperando en La Boheme
para terminar nuestra
partida de ajedrez"
les decía
y ellos le daban
pastillas color
naranja o cielo
que después las tiraba
y en La Boheme
tomandose una cerveza se reía

Benjamín Ferrera
panza de luna llena
y cara de niño necio
como se entristecían sus ojos
al hablar de Cuba
Una noche en un bar me dijo
"Jorgito yo estuve
en Playa Girón
yo defendí la revolución

Recuerdo que cuando
ibamos marchando
hacia el frente
vi los heridos pasar
y sentí miedo
pero no estuve solo en mi miedo
En mi columna todos eramos
muchachos como de catorce años
 y vi en sus ojos el terror.
Pero de pronto alguien gritó
'Cojones que nos quitan
la revolución
-y comenzó a cantar-
Soy comunista
toda la vida
y comunista he de morir'.

Benjamín Ferrera
rebelde con el inglés
y con los gringos
porque decía que tratarlos
de entender era simplemente
una pérdida de tiempo
y mejor bebía
hablaba de Cuba
jugaba a jedrez
o leía a Dostoevsky

Benjamín Ferrera
en una noche
muy muy loca y pasionaria
partió para Mexico
con Victor Hugo
Y Antonio Valencia
Los tres iban borrachos
Benjamín llevaba
lo que le quedaba
de su cheque de loco
los otros que se yo
A los meses dos volvieron
Benjamín no
es que acaso
pudo volver a Cuba
se quedó en México
o se murió

ODE TO BENJAMIN FERRERA

For being honest and making light
of the way he conquered SSI

To avoid work,
Benjamin Ferrera presents himself
as insane
and fools all the psychiatrists
at San Francisco General Hospital
"Karpov is waiting for me
at La Boheme to finish our chess game"
he convinces them
and they give him
pills the color
of oranges or sky
that later he throws away
and at La Boheme
while sipping a beer, he laughs

Benjamin Ferrera
full moon belly
and face of a stubborn child
sadness wells in his eyes
when he remembers Cuba
One evening in a bar
he told me
"Jorgito, I was
in Playa Girón
I defended the revolution
I remember when
we were marching
to the front lines
I saw the wounded pass by
And I was frightened
We were all boys,
in my column,
all about fourteen years old,
and I saw terror in their eyes.
But suddenly someone shouted
 —Cojones, they wanna take
the revolution away from us—
and started to sing,
—I'm a communist for life
and I will die a communist!

Benjamin Ferrera refused
English and the gringos
because he believed
trying to understand them
was a waste of time
So instead he drank
talked about Cuba
played chess
or read Dostoevsky

Benjamin Ferrera
one night
wild and impassioned
left for Mexico
with Antonio Valencia
and Victor Hugo
All three were drunk
Benjamin carrying
what was left
from his loony's check
The others came back
months later
Benjamin did not
Did he return to Cuba,
stay in Mexico,
or did he die?

JORGE RIVERA

Jorge Rivera
alias El Trompudo
Llegó huyendo
desde Cojutepeque
a La Boheme

Un día simplemente
apareció en el café

Pobre trompudo que gran susto
le habrá dado
la guardia salvadoreña
para que sus ojos

aún sigan siendo tan grandes
y espantados

Jorge Rivera
al llegar a La Boheme
no podía decir ni "yes"
pero de susto en susto brincó
a la cama y luego
aprendió inglés

Jorge Rivera ama a El Salvador
y cuando está triste
no llegaba a La Boheme
porque anda conversando
con alguien que aquí nadie conoce
sus amigos que murieron
en El Salvador

JORGE RIVERA

Jorge Rivera,
alias Big Mouth,
fled from the town
q of Cojutepeque
to La Boheme

One day he simply
appeared at the café

Poor Big Mouth!
What a scare
the Salvadoran guard
must have given him
for his eyes
remained so big
so frightened

Jorge Rivera
when he first came
to La Boheme
did not even know
how to say "yes"
But in his fright
he jumped
from bed to bed

and soon
learned all the English
there is to know

Jorge Rivera loves El Salvador
When he is sad
he doesn't come to La Boheme
Instead, he walks around
talking
to those who no one here knows:
his friends, those who died
in El Salvador.

VICTOR MANUEL

Moreno
Delgado
Triste
Pequeño
Amargado
Dulce
Alegre
Confundido

Salió de Cuba
por el Mariel
De allá sólo se trajo
unas botas negras
que arrojo al mar
antes de llegar a Miami

El tatuaje del Che Guevara
que estaba en uno de sus brazos
quién sabe por cuántos años
se lo borró dolorosamente
con sangre
con rabia con amor

Victor,
Inteligente
Sagaz
Tierno
Rudo

Más de alguna vez
le escuché decir
-A esa Boheme
sólo llegan decadentes-

VICTOR MANUEL

Latino
dark
thin
sad
Tiny
embittered
sweet-souled
giddy
confused

He left Cuba
on the ship Mariel
bringing only
a pair of black boots
which he threw into the ocean
before arriving in Miami.

A tattoo of Che Guevara
is on one of his arms
Who knows how many years
he has now erased,
Painfully,
with blood
and rage
and love.

Victor Manuel
intelligent
wise
tender
rude
More than once,
I've heard him say,
"Only the decadent
patronize La Boheme."

DON JOSE

Del viejo José
hay tanto que contar
han sido tantas sus hazañas
que el viejo
es una odisea caminando
De joven jugo futbol
y esto sigue siendo
la única pasión que hay en su vida
Para el mundial de futbol
se ausenta de La Boheme
para evitar
que algún -ignorante-
como él dice
le altere los nervios
El viejo José
hasta hace poco
fumaba poros y se tomaba más
de un vaso de vino
pese a que su doctor
le había recomendado
que no se sobrepasara
A él siempre se le pasaba la mano
Que gran susto
le habrá dado la muerte
le abrieron el pecho
para arreglarle el corazón
Hoy ya no fuma ni bebe
se conforma con hablar de futbol
y contar historias
Entre ellas la del día
que se cayó desde un segundo piso
mientras perseguía
a la mujer que lo traía loco
Pobre viejo José
Mientras jubaba
a las escondidillas con su amor
pensó que abría la puerta de una recámara
pero abrió la de un balcón
El dice no haberse golpeado mucho
porque estaba borracho
y antes de que llegara la ambulancia
subió corriendo para hacer el amor

El viejo José tiene trece años

de llegar a La Boheme
vino desde Argentina
canta tangos no habla Inglés
habla un poco de Italiano
sobre quien lo quiera
El viejo José no sabe
que está loco
ni que está lleno de amor
Yo se que nunca dejará de gritar
ni de reclamar la mejor mesa en La Boheme
Que viva José y los tangos
su locura su amor y La Boheme

DON JOSE

About old José
there's so much to tell
He has had many adventures
The old man
is a walking odyssey
As a boy he played soccer
and it continues to be
the only passion in his life
During the World Cup
he avoids La Boheme
to prevent some –ignoramus-
as he calls them
from getting on his nerves

Old José
Until recently
smoked cigars and drank more
than one glass of wine
despite his doctor's advice
to avoid overindulgence and
He's always crossed the line
Perhaps death
gave him a fright
They opened his chest
to regulate his heart
These days he no longer
smokes or drinks
He finds comfort only in soccer
and in telling stories
among them about the time

he fell from the second story
while chasing
the woman he was crazy for
Poor old José,
while he was playing
hide and seek with his love
thought he was opening the bedroom door
instead he opened the one to the balcony
He said he wasn't hurt
because he was drunk.
And before the ambulance came
he ran back up the stairs
to make love

Old José has been coming
to La Boheme
for thirteen years
He came from Argentina
He sings tangos speaks no English
speaks a little Italian
Old José doesn't know
that he's crazy
nor that he's full of love
I know he'll never stop yelling
nor demanding
the best table in La Boheme
Long live José and the tango
his madness   his love
La Boheme

RICARDITO

Ricardo Ricardito
Filósofo sin filosofia
Niño barbudo
Silencioso en el silencio
que te importa estar solo
en una mesa del café
estás pensando
estás pensando
en un viejo campesino
que se apareció

una mañana en tu casa
allá en Santa Ana
-El señor de los pájaros
Me dijiste con una sonrisa
que más parecía suspiro
-Lo hubieras visto vos Jorge
con una gran jaula
llena de pajaritos
de todos los colores en su hombro
Cuando llegaste a La Boheme
Quien te trajó
No lo digas
no lo grites
dos hermanos
te mataron en El Salvador
Cambiaron las sillas
de La Boheme
el té ya no lo venden
en jarritos de aluminio
las tazas grises de barro
las cambiaron
También La Boheme
cambió de dueño
y vos sentado allí
en una esquina
Pensando
Fresco como una
mañana de invierno
de esas que hay en tu patria
Sereno como si no pasara nada

RICARDITO

Ricardo Ricardito
philosopher without a philosophy
bearded child
silent in the silence
Why is it that you must be alone
at a table in the café?
- Are you thinking
about the old farmhand
who appeared
one morning at your home
in Santa Ana?
"The man of the birds"

you told me with a smile
that seemed more like a sigh.
"You should have seen him, Jorge,
carrying a huge cage on his shoulder,
filled with birds
of all colors."

When you first came to La Boheme
who brought you?
Don't say it.
Don't yell it.
Two brothers,
they killed in El Salvador.

They changed the chairs
of La Boheme.
They don't serve tea
in aluminum teapots
The gray ceramic cups
have been changed.
La Boheme also
changed owners.
And you, sitting there
in the corner, thinking.
Cool as the winter morning
in your country.
Calm,
as if nothing had happened.

AMILCAR CARILLO

Ayer se volvió a ir Amilcar
para Alemania
Amilcar Carrillo y Cabrera
de los de Santa Ana
como él dice cuando está borracho
Amilcar siempre bién vestido
Amilcar hablando con elegancia
Amilcar diciendo en una mesa del café
es la hora alcohólica
a las cinco de la tarde
Amilcar siempre enamorado

siempre conquistando
llevandose las más bonitas
Amilcar siempre puntual en el café
a las tres de la tarde
expreso y vaso con agua

Amilcar no trabaja "no trabajaré para los gringos"
dice en tono intelectual
Amilcar lee libros
piensa
       sueña
se emborracha sin temor a nada
Amilcar sabe ser amigo
                    buén amigo
Amilcar hay quienes no lo quieren
porque no trabaja y viaja
se pasa la vida de los
bares de Hamburgo
a La Boheme
y, además, tiene tres mujeres
que lo aman locamente
Amilcar una vez mientras caminabamos
me dijo "Yo me quisiera llevar
uno de esos pa' Alemania"
señalo un rótulo
de los que se pegan en los parachoques
de los automoviles
en el que se leía
Yo amo El Salvador.

AMILCAR CARRILLO

Yesterday, Amilcar left again for Germany.
"Amilcar Carrillo and Cabrera
from Santa Ana, El Salvador,"
he declares when he's drunk.

Amilcar, always well-dressed
Amilcar, speaking elegantly
Amilcar, announcing from a café table,
"It's Alcoholics' Hour"
at five in the afternoon.
Amilcar, always in love,
always looking,
catching the prettiest.

Amilcar, always punctual at the cafe
at three in the afternoon,
espresso and a glass of water.

Amilcar doesn't work.
"Nor shall I work for the gringos!"
he announces in his intellectual tone of voice.
Amilcar reads books,
thinks dreams.
He gets drunk fearing nothing.

Amilcar knows how to be a friend,
a good friend.
There are some who dislike him
because he travels
without working.
He divides his life
between Hamburg's bars
and La Boheme
and besides, he has three women
who love him madly.

Once, while walking together,
Amilcar nodded at a bumper sticker and said,
"I wish I could take one of those to Germany"
It read: "I Love El Salvador."

ROBINSON TAPIA

Róbinson
está en Francia
y desde que él se fué
La Boheme ya no es la misma

Róbinson Tapia
se cambió el nombre
por Iquique
su pueblo allá
en América del Sur

Róbinson Tapia
loco de buena fé

declamando versos de Gabriela Mistral
cuando borracho
"Ufana con sus colores
volaba la mariposa"

Róbinson Tapia
arquitecto poeta pintor
pero sobre todo loco
decía a gritos
que él no era alcóholico
anónimo,
sino público

Róbinson Tapia,
noble,
hermoso
siempre con las manos llenas
siempre sonriendo
siempre buén amigo

Róbinson Tapia
Algún dia volverá
para que La Boheme
vuelva a ser Boheme

ROBINSON TAPIA

Robinson is in France
and since he left
La Boheme is not the same.

Robinson Tapia,
changed his name
to Iquique
his hometown
in South America.

Robinson Tapia,
good-humored madman,
recited Gabriela Mistral's poems
while drunk:
"Proud with its colors
flies the butterfly"

Robinson Tapia

architect, poet, painter
but above all else, a crazed free-spirit.
He shouts
he's not an alcoholic anonymous,
he's a public one.

Robinson Tapia,
noble
beautiful
always with open arms
always smiling
always a good friend.

Robinson Tapia
One day he will return,
so La Boheme
will become La Boheme once again.

CORAZÓN DEL BARRIO

Las calles
Del barrio La Mission
Son venas tropicales
El sabor de la fruta
Sabe a nuestro continente

Los Mangos
Las Sandías
Las Papayas
Los Melones

Caminar por estas calles
Es como estar
En el pecho de América
O simplemente
Vivir en un barrio que tiene corazón

HEART OF THE NEIGHBORHOOD

The streets
of the Mission District

are tropical veins
the flavor of fruit
that taste of our continent

The Mangos
The Watermelons
The Papayas
The Melons

To walk through these streets
is like coming to
the chest of America
or simply
living in a neighborhood that has a heart

ABOUT THE AUTHORS

JOIE COOK is the author of many small press publications. The poems included in *Acts of Submission* previously appeared in *Cash for Color TVs*, *Public Tragedies*, *Ecto-Gyno*, *The Vacancy Within*, and *Twenty-Four Hours of Years*. She currently lives in Southern California.

BUCKY SINISTER is the author of *King of the Roadkills* (Manic D Press). For many years, he ran the infamous poetry readings at the Chameleon in San Francisco. His work has appeared in *The Outlaw Bible of American Poetry* (Thunders Mouth) and many other publications.

NANCY DEPPER is a former member of the San Francisco Poetry Slam team. Her work has appeared in several anthologies, including *Signs of Life* (Manic D Press). Her writing was nominated for a Pushcart Prize in 1999. She lives in Seattle.

SPARROW 13 is the author of *Hell Soup: The Collected Writings of Sparrow 13 LaughingWand* (Manic D Press). He lives in San Francisco.

MICHELE C. lives in San Francisco.

JERRY D. MILEY was awarded a 1995 Mary Tall Mountain Creative Writing and Community Service Award. He ran the Tenderloin Recreation and Education Center's People's Library from 1991-96.

WENDY-O MATIK is the author of *Love Like Rage* (Manic D Press). Her work has appeared in dozens of small magazines and anthologies, and she has performed her work at readings throughout the U.S. Her work appears on the benefit CD *Home Alive* (Epic Records). She lives in Berkeley, California.

DAVID JEWELL is the author of *Lizards Again* (Manic D Press). He has released several spoken word recordings, and his work has appeared in Richard Linklater's film *Before Sunrise*. He lives in Austin, Texas.

JENNIFER JOSEPH is the author of *The Future Isn't What It Used To Be* (Manic D Press). Her writing has appeared in many anthologies including *Sisters of the Extreme* (Inner Traditions).

LISA RADON is the author of *The Super Deluxe With Everything* (Big Star Press), and *It's All Fun And Games Until Somebody Loses An Eye* (Big Star Press). She's written three pieces for performance by multiple voices including *Five Feet High and Rising*, which was funded in part by a grant from the Santa Cruz City Arts Commission. She currently lives in the Pacific Northwest.

JON LONGHI is the author of *Flashbacks and Premonitions* (Manic D Press), *The Rise and Fall of Third Leg* (Manic D Press), and *Bricks and Anchors* (Manic D Press). He has read his work all over the U.S. He lives in San Francisco.

JORGE ARGUETA is the author of many books, including the award-winning children's book *A Movie In My Pillow* (Children's Book Press). A native of El Salvador, he lives in San Francisco.

Manic D Press Books

In the Small of My Backyard. Matt Cook. $13.95
Monster Fashion. Jarret Keene. $13.95
This Too Can Be Yours. Beth Lisick. $13.95
Devil Babe's Big Book of Postcards. Isabel Samaras. $11.95
Harmless Medicine. Justin Chin. $13.95
Depending on the Light. Thea Hillman. $13.95
Escape from Houdini Mountain. Pleasant Gehman. $13.95
Poetry Slam: the competitive art of performance poetry. Gary Glazner, ed. $15
I Married An Earthling. Alvin Orloff. $13.95
Cottonmouth Kisses. Clint Catalyst. $12.95
Fear of A Black Marker. Keith Knight. $11.95
Red Wine Moan. Jeri Cain Rossi. $11.95
Dirty Money and other stories. Ayn Imperato. $11.95
Sorry We're Close. J. Tarin Towers. $11.95
Po Man's Child: a novel. Marci Blackman. $12.95
The Underground Guide to Los Angeles. Pleasant Gehman, ed. $14.95
The Underground Guide to San Francisco. Jennifer Joseph, ed. $14.95
Flashbacks and Premonitions. Jon Longhi. $11.95
The Forgiveness Parade. Jeffrey McDaniel. $11.95
The Sofa Surfing Handbook. Juliette Torrez, ed. $11.95
Abolishing Christianity and other short pieces. Jonathan Swift. $11.95
Growing Up Free In America. Bruce Jackson. $11.95
Devil Babe's Big Book of Fun! Isabel Samaras. $11.95
Dances With Sheep. Keith Knight. $11.95
Monkey Girl. Beth Lisick. $11.95
Bite Hard. Justin Chin. $11.95
Next Stop: Troubletown. Lloyd Dangle. $10.95
The Hashish Man and other stories. Lord Dunsany. $11.95
Forty Ouncer. Kurt Zapata. $11.95
The Unsinkable Bambi Lake. Bambi Lake with Alvin Orloff. $11.95
Hell Soup: the collected writings of Sparrow 13 LaughingWand. $8.95
The Ghastly Ones & Other Fiendish Frolics. Richard Sala. $9.95
King of the Roadkills. Bucky Sinister. $9.95
Alibi School. Jeffrey McDaniel. $11.95
Signs of Life: channel-surfing through '90s culture. Joseph, ed. $12.95
Beyond Definition. Blackman & Healey, eds. $10.95
The Rise and Fall of Third Leg. Jon Longhi. $9.95
Specimen Tank. Buzz Callaway. $10.95
The Verdict Is In. edited by Kathi Georges & Jennifer Joseph. $9.95
The Back of a Spoon. Jack Hirschman. $7
Baroque Outhouse/Decapitated Head of a Dog. Randolph Nae. $7
Graveyard Golf and other stories. Vampyre Mike Kassel. $7.95
Bricks and Anchors. Jon Longhi. $8
Greatest Hits. edited by Jennifer Joseph. $7
Lizards Again. David Jewell. $7
The Future Isn't What It Used To Be. Jennifer Joseph. $7

Please add $4 to all orders for postage and handling.
Manic D Press • Box 410804 • San Francisco CA 94141 USA
info@manicdpress.com   www.manicdpress.com